BLACK AND BLUE

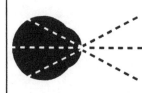

This Large Print Book carries the
Seal of Approval of N.A.V.H.

BLACK AND BLUE

DAVID ROSENFELT

THORNDIKE PRESS
A part of Gale, a Cengage Company

Farmington Hills, Mich • San Francisco • New York • Waterville, Maine
Meriden, Conn • Mason, Ohio • Chicago

Copyright © 2019 by Tara Productions, Inc.
A Doug Brock Thriller.
Thorndike Press, a part of Gale, a Cengage Company.

Thorndike Press® Large Print Core.
The text of this Large Print edition is unabridged.
Other aspects of the book may vary from the original edition.
Set in 16 pt. Plantin.

LIBRARY OF CONGRESS CIP DATA ON FILE.
CATALOGUING IN PUBLICATION FOR THIS BOOK
IS AVAILABLE FROM THE LIBRARY OF CONGRESS

ISBN-13: 978-1-4328-7041-6 (hardcover alk. paper)

Published in 2019 by arrangement with Macmillan Publishing Group, LLC/St. Martin's Press

Printed in Mexico
1 2 3 4 5 6 7 23 22 21 20 19

BLACK AND BLUE

I feel like a jerk.

It's been happening quite often lately; it seems to go with my relatively new territory. It bothered me a lot at first, but I've started to get used to it. I might as well, because there's no way around it.

First, a little background. My name is Doug Brock. I'm a cop, a lieutenant in the homicide division of the New Jersey State Police. A while back I was shot and suffered a head injury that left me with retrograde amnesia.

I made it back to work, and it is understating the case to say that I got revenge on the guy who shot me. Whereas I lost the last ten years of my life, at least in terms of my memory, he lost the rest of his life. I guess since I lost the past and he lost the future, you could say I won, but it's close.

I've actually made some progress . . . recovered some memories. I would estimate maybe half, although since I don't know what I don't know, it's hard to be sure.

That's the good news. The bad news is that I stopped retrieving lost memories about six months ago, and my neurologist tells me that I'm probably finished. You can't jog memories that aren't there, and for me, many of them have left the building. I'm trying not to be bitter about it, with intermittent success.

Creating new memories is not a problem, fortunately. Of course, the downside is that this means I can remember the fact that there is much I can't remember. I am living the song lyric, "Like the circles that you find, in the windmills of your mind."

So the annoyances can be major, like when I learn that I've forgotten some significant event in my life. Or they can be minor, like a few minutes ago, when my memory loss made me feel like a jerk.

Again.

My girlfriend, Jessie Allen, or my almost-fiancée, Jessie Allen, depending on her mood, asked me to pick up some stuff for dinner at the supermarket. So that's where I am right now, standing about halfway down a long aisle, looking for flavored water.

Jessie's preferred flavor is blueberry, although I have confirmed by conducting my own personal tests that they all taste the same. Yet despite this, people swear by their own favorites. In this they are much like M&M's; on some level I recognize that the different colors are indistinguishable by taste, yet I am devoted to the blue ones.

But regarding the water — I, as a cop, am suspicious of the entire thing. The label says that there are no calories, fat, sodium, protein, or anything; then what the hell are they adding to the water to give it the taste?

About thirty seconds ago a woman turned the corner into the aisle, pushing a cart. She brightened when she looked my way and said, "Doug! Hi! It's been so long!"

She was probably in her late twenties, wearing a T-shirt and sweatpants, probably stopping off on the way to the gym. Her next stop was likely going to be the produce aisle to buy vegetables to help maintain the clearly excellent body those gym stops had produced. Her idea of a decadent dessert is probably dipping actual blueberries in fake blueberry water.

But all in all, definitely a woman I could have known in my now partially erased past.

Since I didn't remember her, I went into my fake-recognition routine. It's one I have gotten quite proficient at. "Hi! Boy it sure has been a long time, but it's great to see you. How's everything?"

"What?" she asked, somehow not understanding what the hell I was talking about. Then the realization hit me, and I turned around to see another guy behind me, waving to the woman and simultaneously looking at me like I'm nuts.

I am nuts, but I'm also a cop, so I could have come up with a pretense to ask for his ID, but I'd pretty much bet anything that his name is also Doug. When I looked back, the woman was looking at me just as strangely.

My only effective way to minimize the embarrassment of the situation would have been to shoot them both, but that seemed like literal overkill, so instead I just wheeled my cart out of the aisle in humiliation and let T-shirt lady and Doug reminisce without me.

As I head toward the checkout lane without the flavored water, I am surprised to see my partner, Nate Alvarez, standing there. I can only assume that Jessie told him I was here; otherwise he is doing a really bad job of secret surveillance.

Nate is six seven, two hundred and eighty pounds. He is constantly on a diet, and those diets are constantly failing. "Chocolate covered cherries are in aisle three," I say.

He frowns. "Wiseass. Let's go."

"Let's go where?"

"To work."

"Today is our day off. . . . I'm going to barbecue."

"What are you making? Tofu burgers? Wheat germ steaks?" Nate is a bit disdainful of Jessie's attempts, with occasional success, to get me to eat healthier.

"Salmon."

He frowns again, as if the very concept of salmon is distasteful. "I'm not surprised. Let's go."

"Why?"

"I'll tell you on the way. We'll take my car and get yours later."

"Where are we going?" I ask when we're in the car.

"Eastside Park in Paterson. There's a dead body waiting for us."

"Who is it?"

He shrugs. "I don't know yet. White male, forties; the son of a bitch apparently doesn't care that you were having a barbecue party today. By the way, why didn't you invite me?"

"First of all, it isn't a party. Just Jessie and me. And besides, the last time we had you over for dinner you blew a huge hole in our food budget. You even ate three of the plates. We had to eat porridge from a bowl for six months."

"What the hell is porridge, anyway? Like a soup?" Nate asks.

"Nothing like a soup. But you'd like it; just put chocolate syrup on it. Why are we getting this call on our day off?"

"By any chance does the name Walter Brookings mean anything to you?"

I hate these kind of questions, because I really hate not being able to remember things. Based on the way Nate asked the question, I have a feeling this is a name I'm supposed to recall. It sounds vaguely familiar, but I'm reaching for the memory and coming up with nothing.

Rather than going into the routine where I pretend to remember and hope to figure it out in the conversation, I say, "No. Not at the moment."

Nate frowns. "Wow. I never would have guessed it."

"Who is he?"

"Who was he is the better question."

"Fine. So who was he?"

We're pulling into Eastside Park, and there are a bunch of cop cars near the tennis courts. A media truck has arrived already; I have no doubt there will be others soon. Murder scenes give off a scent that attracts them.

There is a common look and feel to situations like this; I've seen a lot of them. There's always a great deal of action and energy, everybody is always moving, except the victim.

Nate parks nearby and says, "I'll tell you

about Brookings later. If we're lucky it won't even matter."

We get out and I notice that the scene is being managed by the Paterson cops. The head of their homicide division, Captain Pete Stanton, is running the show, and Paterson forensics is on the case. That's all fine with me; I know Stanton and like him, and he's a thoroughly competent cop. I've never had any issues with their forensics people either.

Of course, since the body has been found in a Paterson park, next to a Paterson tennis court, it's no surprise that they're here. What puzzles me is why we're here, but I guess I'll find that out later, when I learn about Walter Brookings.

Pete must be wondering the same thing because he comes over as soon as he sees us. "What the hell are you two doing here? You don't have jurisdiction, and you're not really dressed for tennis." Then he looks at Nate's body and says, "You're not really built for it either."

"We're just making sure you guys don't screw up," Nate says. "That's a full-time job in itself."

"You think this is tied into Brookings?"

"We wait for you local guys to tell us what to think," Nate says, and then points to me.

"Memory Boy here doesn't even remember Brookings."

Pete says to me, "Do you remember that your fat partner is an asshole?"

I nod. "That's a new memory I form every day."

"So is it tied to Brookings or not?" Nate asks.

"Beats the shit out of me, but there are similarities," Pete says. "High-powered rifle, one shot in the heart from distance. Too soon to know much more, but it wouldn't surprise me."

As he says, "from distance," he points to a wooded area about a hundred yards away. It's a difficult shot from there, but not impossible.

"The Brookings shot was a lot tougher," Nate says. "But it certainly seems similar."

"If it's the same guy, he's been quiet for a long time. But it's also too long for a copycat."

Based on all of this, my easy assumption is that this Brookings guy was shot in a similar fashion to this victim. We probably investigated that case, and the possible connection is the reason we're here for what should be a local case. But Brookings apparently was shot a fairly long time ago.

It would be nice if I didn't have to analyze

clues to piece together my own damn life.

We head over to get a look at the body, a perk reserved for us lucky few. Pete walks with us and on the way says that the victim is Alex Randowsky. At this point all they have to go on is his driver's license and some credit cards, although his tennis partner is being interviewed, which will obviously reveal much more.

Within an hour they will have a treasure trove of information on Alex Randowsky, but the most important fact is that he is lying on the Eastside Park grass with a bullet in his chest.

For now, based on the fact that he was carrying an American Express Platinum Card, we know he probably had money. The driver's license provides the data to be used in locating next of kin, and also indicates that he was an organ donor.

One of the organs he definitely won't be donating is his heart, because a bullet has gone directly through it. No matter where the murderer stood, it is clear that he is a very good shot.

Randowsky is wearing tennis clothes and there is a racquet lying next to the body. Since he's come to rest about ten feet from the court, it's a pretty good bet he was there to play tennis. Another pretty good bet is that his tennis career is over.

"Who was he playing with?" I ask.

Pete just points toward a group of people on the other side of the court, where police are questioning another guy of similar age, also in tennis clothes.

Once Pete agrees to forward us all relevant forensic information and witness statements, Nate and I have nothing else to do here, so we leave. Nate is going to drive me back to my car, but first he calls in to our immediate boss, Captain Bradley, to update him on the little we learned. If Bradley is involved at this point, this is high priority.

Nate tells him the basics, and then Bradley must ask about Brookings, because Nate says, "No way to tell yet; maybe ballistics will help. It's been a while since Brookings, but if it's a different perp, then there's two damn good shooters out there."

Another pause, after which Nate answers, "He doesn't remember Brookings." A beat, and then, "Tell me about it."

Nate hangs up, so it's my turn to say, "Now you tell me about it."

"Brookings was a Boy Scout," Nate says.

"Pure as the driven snow?" I ask, since "Boy Scout" is a term we use for such people.

"No, I mean literally a Boy Scout. In his spare time he was a troop leader, or captain, or whatever the hell they're called. Guy lived in a fancy house, but he went into the woods and slept in a tent and roasted marshmallows. Stuff like that never makes sense to me, except for the marshmallow part."

"I assume that's not why he was killed."

Nate shakes his head. "I doubt it, but we never did come up with a reason or a decent suspect. When he wasn't telling campfire stories to ten-year-olds, he owned a carton factory in Totowa. It's still there; probably employs two hundred people."

"Sounds rich."

"Very, and he wasn't shy about giving it

18

away. Ate a lot of chicken at a lot of charity dinners. Definitely in the model-citizen category. I'd want my son to be like him, if he wasn't dead. And if I had a son."

"First you might want to get a date. But Brookings was shot?" I ask. "One bullet through the heart?"

He nods. "Right. Leaving one of those dinners, as a matter of fact. It was at the Brownstone."

"What's the Brownstone?"

Nate gives me that annoyed look that tells me I should know this. It's been a while since he's been sensitive to my feelings about my memory loss. Sensitivity isn't Nate's strong point; actually, I'm not that big on it either.

"It's a place downtown that does weddings, dinners, that kind of stuff."

"Have I ever been there?" I ask, and then regret it immediately.

"What am I, your diary? But you probably haven't; it's a classy place. Anyway, he was shot coming out of there after a dinner. We figured out where the shot came from; it was about three hundred yards in the dark. Not exactly a drive-by, you know?"

"When was this?"

"Maybe eighteen months ago — or less. I'd have to check."

"No wonder," I say, but I don't elaborate, because I don't have to. Nate knows what I mean. Eighteen months would place it about four months before I was shot and lost most of ten years of my life. The most recent memories are the ones I have most consistently lost, so I'm not surprised that this is one of them.

He continues. "Anyway, you and I drew the case, but basically the whole unit was on it. There was no obvious reason that anyone would kill Brookings. He didn't seem to have an enemy in the world, so everybody was afraid it was going to start a bunch of random killings. Like that sniper case in DC."

I have no idea what sniper case in DC he might be talking about, but there's no upside in my asking. "But it was a one-off? No more shootings?"

He nods. "Right. So after a while, it died down. We had a few suspects, but none we ever considered good enough."

"What was the weapon?"

"M4. I can tell you this; if ballistics matches this to Brookings, the shit is going to hit the fan."

I nod. "Tune in tomorrow."

Nate drops me back at the supermarket, and I go in to buy the stuff I left in the cart before. At least this time I won't have to see the woman who knows the other Doug. But I might run into somebody else I should know; the supermarket is a scary place.

Jessie is home when I get there. We are living together, which in itself is a minor miracle. It would be fair to say that our relationship has developed in a rather unusual manner. We dated and got engaged, which was a good start. Then I went through a difficult emotional time because someone I cared about was killed. I blamed myself and pushed everyone away — especially Jessie.

To put it in her terms, I dumped her.

Then I lost my memory, and since she is a cop stationed in the same precinct as me, I met her again, as if for the first time. I had no recollection of our previous time together, but she definitely did. She remembered every excruciating detail.

I fell for her again, probably because she's beautiful and smart and funny. Unfortunately, she still hated me for having hurt her. I worked hard to overcome that, but it has taken her an understandably long time to regain her trust in me. When she looks into the future, she has difficulty not seeing the past.

Jessie usually takes small steps toward letting me earn back that trust, but allowing me to move back in with her was a huge one. The fact that she insisted I keep my apartment, just in case, was a condition I was happy to live with. In fact, I'm happy to live with any conditions she sets, because I'm happy to live with her.

Speaking of living with, we share the house with her dog, Bobo. Bobo is black, very hairy, and enormous. I think he's a Newfoundland/tractor-trailer mix. More significantly, he doesn't like me.

I've never done anything to him that could come close to justifying that attitude. I often feed him and take him for walks, though the truth is it would be easier to use a saddle than a leash. I always make it a point to smile when I'm around him, although it's always an uneasy smile.

But he barely tolerates me; he makes that clear. And he often physically gets between Jessie and me, which is not a good thing. I understand he's being protective of her, and he takes that assignment very seriously. At least Bobo hasn't hurt me, and he hasn't eaten me, so all is not yet lost.

It's late already, so we decide to freeze the barbecue stuff and order in a pizza. If there is one truth I have learned, and more importantly never forgotten, it's that it is never a bad idea to order in a pizza.

While we're waiting for it to arrive, Jessie pours herself a glass of wine, hands me a beer, and asks, "Is it tied in to Brookings?"

"Don't know yet. So you remember Brookings?" I ask. "Were you on the case?" Jessie is now head of the computer division at the precinct, but she used to be on the street. That's where she would still rather be, but she has been a victim of her technology expertise. In the new world, being in charge of cyber-stuff pretty much makes her the lead detective in the unit, but she doesn't see it that way.

"Yes. It was all hands on deck; the pressure was on. You don't remember it?"

"No; it happened in my dark period. But Nate has been updating me, between insults."

"If this is the same perp," she says, "we're in for a wild ride." Then, "Probably will be a wild ride either way."

The first thing I do when I get in this morning is call up the file on Brookings.

Nate is not here yet; Jessie and I always drive in together really early. She likes to get a lot of work in before the phone starts ringing, and I like to inhale a lot of coffee and donuts before the real work starts. It's a different approach, but both of our methods seem to work.

Obviously, there is no compelling need to familiarize myself with Brookings yet; the ballistics aren't in. But there's also no harm in it either. I'd like to know more about it, especially what my actions were.

This is not the first time I've gone back and checked out a cold case to see what steps I took. It's a weird feeling when I do it, like reading a novel about my own life without knowing what comes next. But it can be good or bad; I cringe at the prospect of seeing that I did something wrong, and

I'm very relieved on the occasions that I'm pleased by my performance. I'm rather self-critical, so I do a lot more cringing than smiling.

In the Brookings case, I'm also hoping to see something with fresh eyes. It's an open case, though growing cold, so it would be nice to find the killer regardless of whether he has struck again.

Since Nate and I are homicide detectives, finding killers is actually part of our job description.

We've been having pretty good success lately, having cleared three cases in the last three weeks. They haven't been head scratchers; the likely suspects all but screamed their guilt at us. One of them was still at the scene, the murder weapon in his hands. That's usually a pretty good clue.

But the point is we've arrested all three, and put neat cases in the hands of the prosecutors.

It's a great feeling, one I will never get tired of.

The only recent open case that Nate and I are working on is a domestic murder; a woman by the name of Nina Muller was brutally murdered while she slept alone in her rented Passaic apartment.

We were called in on this one because

there was more than one county involved. Mrs. Muller and her husband, Frank, lived in Englewood, and their life there did not go smoothly, primarily because Frank is a violent, abusive scumbag.

The Englewood police were called in on numerous occasions by Mrs. Muller because Frank was abusing her. She finally summoned the guts to move out, and she took the Passaic apartment on a temporary basis, the first step in starting a new life. Frank threatened her, and she went to court and received a restraining order against him. She told the judge that she feared for her life.

There is little question that the restraining order did not restrain Frank at all, and that he's the one who broke into her apartment and stabbed her to death. There is no evidentiary doubt of that; she fought back and had his skin under her fingernails. Frank took off and hasn't been seen since.

We've put out the word, and he will be found; the only question is when. I'm hoping to be the one to find him, and I'm hoping he will resist arrest.

I open the Brookings file and begin reading. There is a lot of biographical stuff on Brookings, and he is mostly as Nate had described him. He was rich, no doubt about that, and he was also philanthropic. A wing at Hackensack University Medical Center is named after him; an unpleasant irony is that's where he was declared dead after being shot.

Brookings was forty-nine and left a wife and two adult children behind. There is very little in the files about the kids; they live out of state.

The phone rings and it is Captain Bradley on the other line. "Get your ass in here," he says. Captain Bradley is not much of a chit-chatter; I like that about him.

As I'm walking out of the office, Nate is walking in. "Where are you going?"

"Bradley. He told me to get my ass into his office."

"What about me?"

"He didn't mention anything about your ass. He might consider it too large; he doesn't have that big an office. If we were meeting in the conference room, that would be a different story."

Nate doesn't seem deterred by that and follows me toward Bradley's office. There's no doubt Bradley wants both of us; when it comes to investigations, Nate and I have long been joined at the hip, if not the ass.

When we enter Bradley's office, the first thing he says is, "Close the door." But as he says it, he is walking over and closing it himself. Once he does, he gets right to the point. "I just got off the phone with Captain Stanton from Paterson PD. The ballistics report is on the way to us, but he was giving us a heads-up. It's a match to Brookings."

"Shit," Nate says.

Bradley turns to me. "I understand you don't remember Brookings?"

"I'm reading up on it."

"Good; read fast. Because we are full-out on this one."

"Do we go public with the match?" I ask.

"Opinions, please." It is Bradley's style to seek input before making a key decision, a technique I respect. He doesn't always agree, which is fine.

Nate shakes his head. "I say we sit on it, at least for a while. We'd just scare people; there will be plenty of time for that later."

"I don't agree," I say. "It's going to come out anyway, and then we'll look bad for concealing it. But more importantly, the public has a right to know, and they might even help. We are going to have to find a connection between Brookings and Randowsky, and maybe someone will come forward with it."

Bradley nods. "Okay. I'm inclined to agree with Doug, but I'll think more about it. And

I want to talk to the commissioner. What I really want to do is hold a press conference to announce an arrest, so get working on making that happen."

There is one highly unusual aspect to the case which jumps out at us.

Why would the killer wait eighteen months between shootings?

"Maybe he was in jail," Nate says. "Or hurt. Or out of the country."

Of those choices, jail seems the most likely, and it's something we will follow up on immediately. But a lot of people go in and out of jails every day, and there is no guarantee that our guy was incarcerated anywhere around here. That means the suspect pool would be a very large one.

Of course, we are looking for a guy who went away soon after Brookings, and got out relatively recently, so that narrows it down a bit more. But there will still be a lot of people who fit within that time frame.

The possibilities that Nate mentioned make sense if this is truly a random series of murders. If it comes from nothing but the excitement of killing, then eighteen months would be a superhuman time to wait. It would mean that the thrill-killer is demonstrating a deliberateness beyond anything I've ever encountered. The only way that would seem possible would be if the killer were literally unable to act, for reasons like incarceration or injury.

Of course, there is always the possibility that the killer actually has struck in the interim, possibly in a different jurisdiction using a different tactic and weapon. For example, had he strangled a jogger in a park in Newark, we'd have had no reason to tie it to Brookings.

There is also the definite chance that it's not random at all, that Randowsky and Brookings were connected, and that the motive for their murders isn't yet apparent. That motive, whatever it may be, might contain within it an explanation for the unusually long time between the killings.

Obviously we've only started to scratch the surface on Randowsky, so it's way too soon to make any judgments. But Jessie and her staff are already in the process of doing a deep dive to learn everything about him that we can online. Interviews with friends, family, and business associates will give us a much more detailed and accurate picture, but the online search is a big help to start us off.

Randowsky was a lawyer and partner in a Ridgewood firm that practices mostly family law. He was forty-five years old, and divorced with no children. There is also some indication that he was well off financially, and gave time and money to charitable efforts.

There is no obvious connection to Brookings other than their common wealth and willingness to help others. But there are many ways a rich businessman and a lawyer could be linked, and we will track down all the possibilities.

But for now all we know is that someone obviously smart and painstaking, and a deadly marksman to boot, is lying in wait and shooting people for a reason still to be explained.

So all I can do is go back to reading. A lot of the legwork on Brookings has obviously already been done, some of it by me. Even though it never led to anything positive, at the very least it's valuable as a guide to prevent us having to go down the same unproductive roads again.

Nate joins me in going through the files; it's been a while and he's not as up on it as he'll need to be. I'm glad he's doing so, because I can ask him questions about some of the information, since he might be familiar with some of the nuances that are not written down.

After about ten minutes, he says, "You know, we could do this just as well in the cafeteria."

I nod. "I'm sure we could. But all the files are here, on the third floor. The cafeteria is downstairs, on the first floor. It's a two-floor difference."

"I know where the cafeteria is, wiseass. We can take the files with us. Reading makes me hungry."

"Everything makes you hungry. Eating makes you hungry."

"Beating the shit out of you is going to leave me famished." He stands up, grabbing some files as he does. "I'll be reading in the cafeteria."

With Nate gone and me not having to listen to his stomach making noises, I can actually concentrate better. Once I'm finished with the Brookings bio material, I can get into the substance of the investigation.

It is immediately obvious that the department went into a full-court press on this. Nate and I actually split up and interviewed potential witnesses and suspects separately, a sure sign that we wanted to maximize manpower and speed things up.

Also, since we were in charge, one of us often had to stay back at our desk going through the reports the other cops were filing. That's going to happen again as the current case heats up. Neither of us will be happy about it, but it is unavoidable.

A total of four hundred and forty-one interview reports were submitted, from all the members of the department. Either my signature or Nate's is on every one of them; as leaders of the investigation it was important that we see everything, and the signatures show that we did.

I've been through things like this so many times that it shouldn't be stunning to me that I remember none of it, but it still seems hard to believe.

And it is very, very frustrating.

I call Jessie and ask her to have her people run down everyone mentioned in these files to determine if any of them were out of commission for the last eighteen months. It's a long shot, but necessary. She's already working on possible connections between Brookings and Randowsky, but says she'll have the team get to it as soon as they can.

I grab some files and head to the cafeteria to join Nate. Being frustrated makes me hungry.

Nate and I head back to Eastside Park.

We've been to the crime scene already, but it was in the middle of the chaos after the discovery of the body. At the time we didn't even know if we'd be on the case; it wasn't yet tied in to Brookings. This will give us more of a chance to get a feel for what happened and how.

The area is still roped off, and there are three Paterson cops guarding the perimeter. The media trucks are gone and there is no commotion, but the event will certainly live on in the memory of those who were here. It will be at least a couple of days before anyone can play tennis here again, and probably a lot longer before many people would have the guts.

I'm sure the cops have been told to let us in, and they do so after following the proper procedure of making us show our badges. Obviously the body has been removed, but we head to where it was found.

Based on the witness interview that the Paterson cops conducted with Randowsky's tennis partner, they had just finished playing on court three. The way the courts are set up, the exit for the caged-in courts is at the side of court one, so Randowsky and his partner would have walked past courts one and two, no doubt well behind the baselines so as not to have interfered with play.

Of course, it's possible the other two courts were not being used, but we don't know that yet. We'll find that out when we conduct our own interview with Randowsky's partner, or read the interviews the Paterson cops conducted.

Once he exited the playing area, Randowsky walked about ten feet, probably toward where his car was parked. At that point he was also walking toward the woods in the distance, and that is when he was shot. He was facing his executioner, but did not know that. In fact, he probably never realized it; he was dead before he hit the ground.

"Shooter picked the perfect time," Nate says.

I nod. "Right, and not by accident. He had to be lying in wait. Randowsky was heading toward him, so it was a direct shot. The fact that he was walking wasn't a problem, because he was walking head on into the bullet."

"You could have made that shot," Nate says. I ignore the insult; we both know that I could be woken up out of a dead sleep and outshoot Nate. "He could have shot him earlier, while he was playing," Nate continues. "There's a lot of down time in tennis when you're not moving . . . between points."

"But then he'd have been shooting through this chain link fence. No sense doing that if he knew which way Randowsky would be coming once they were done. And he certainly knew, because this is the only way out, and the shooter probably knew where he was parked. It's not like the shooter was waiting on a busy street; he had all the time in the world, without any real concern about being seen."

Nate nods. "And he probably didn't pick up the weapon until it was almost time, so if somehow he was seen earlier, he could have just aborted."

We walk toward the woods where the shooter must have been hidden. I mentally count the paces I take, although it's really not necessary. The tech people have identified where the shot likely came from, and they measured the distance as one hundred and twenty yards. An easy shot for anyone with experience with the M4 rifle, the weapon that was used.

The shooting site is taped off, and it's not necessary for us to enter the small area. It's only about six feet by five feet, and it's set about five feet into the woods. The shooter chose perfectly; he was concealed while he waited for Randowsky to finish, but had a good enough sight line to make the shot.

There are indentations in the grass where the shooter set up; I doubt they reveal his shoe type or weight. I make a note to find out if anybody is already trying to figure that out; knowing Pete Stanton, I am sure the Paterson cops are working on it. But if not, we will, though it's likely that nothing will come of it.

"Okay," Nate says. "He fired the shot. Now what?"

It's a question I had already started thinking about. "The woods go back about forty yards, all the way out to Derrom Avenue. He could have parked there, but there would be signs of him walking in that direction, to and from the car. Some footprints, maybe some broken shrubs; the report from the Paterson cops says they didn't find any.

Still, it's possible."

"Seems risky to have left his car there."

I nod. "Especially since there could easily have been people on that street; it's a neighborhood. He'd be walking out of the woods, which is not an everyday occurrence; he would know that someone might take notice of it."

"And he'd be carrying a rifle, though probably in some kind of case."

I think about it for a while. We're dealing with a shrewd and careful guy; walking out of the woods into possible witnesses just doesn't make sense. "I think he walked this way," I say, pointing toward the courts.

"Takes a shot and then walks out of the woods and toward the scene where everyone can see him?"

"Think about it. A shot is fired; a loud noise, and probably no one knows what it was. But Randowsky goes down, people are screaming, and there is blood everywhere. Nobody has any idea where the shooter is; if they're clearheaded at all, they're seeking cover."

"So he walks out and acts like one of the scared people," Nate says.

"And if he's smart, which he obviously is, he's wearing tennis clothes and the rifle is in a racquet case. The M4 folds up; it would fit in easily. Then he gets in the car and drives away, probably that way, since he'd figure the police are going to enter through the main entrance. But he'd be gone long before they got here anyway."

"We are dealing with one cold-blooded son of a bitch," Nate says. "A cold-blooded son of a bitch who can shoot."

I nod. "Those are the worst kind."

We head back to the station. I spend the time thinking about motive. Until now I've thought there were two possibilities. One, that Randowsky and Brookings have some still to be discovered connection — also tied in to the killer — and that explains why they were the two targets. The other was that these are just random shootings by a determined but deranged individual.

Now I see a third possibility that combines the first two: Brookings and Randowsky could, in fact, have been chosen randomly — meaning that the killer had no particular grudge against them, or reason to kill them. But the point is they were chosen; that much is certain.

The shooter in the park was waiting for Randowsky; there were plenty of other people he could have killed. So Randowsky may have been chosen at random, but he was chosen in advance, and he was specifically targeted. Just the fact that the shooter seemed to have known what car Randowsky was driving and where he was parked lends credence to this argument.

When we get back, it's almost four o'clock. I figure I'll read more of the file for a couple of hours, and then leave. Jessie will probably be home before me, so she'll have walked Bobo and then started dinner. I'm hoping pizza, but I probably won't get my wish.

There are a few pieces of mail on my desk, one of which attracts my attention. It's a plain white envelope, addressed to me, in large print letters. There's no return address, which is what seems strange.

I have pretty good instincts on things like this, and my gut is telling me that this envelope is worrisome. I should take it down to the lab to have them look at it; for all I know there could be anthrax in there. But that's not my style, so I open it carefully, slitting the edge so as not to interfere with it too much.

There's a piece of paper inside, folded over once. It is a short message, in the same block letters as the address on the outside. It says:

"Ninety-seven creeps on the wall. If one

"That note says a lot," Jessie says.

We've just finished our barbecue dinner, a day late, and we've followed our rule of not talking business during the meal. It took a lot of willpower to stick to that this time, and once the last dish is put away, Jessie jumps right into it. I think I know where she's going with this, but I don't interrupt.

"First of all," she continues, "that 'on the wall' game always starts with ninety-nine, so if there are ninety-six left it means there's a third murder we don't know about, which in turn means he is not always using the same MO with the same rifle. Because if he was, we would know about it, no matter where it happened."

"Unless the victim's body wasn't found."

She shakes her head. "Very unlikely. This note means he's bragging. You don't conceal something if you're going to brag about it. Not only is he not deliberately concealing it, but he's actually announcing it."

"I agree," I say. "So if there is a third victim, it means maybe he hasn't been away or inactive for the eighteen months; there has been a murder in the interim."

She nods her agreement and continues. "It also demonstrates that he's not finished, which I suppose we could have figured out anyway. There are, in his mind, ninety-seven more victims to fall."

"There's one other thing," I say. "I think it's significant that he addressed the note to me."

"How so?"

"I'm just one of a group of us working it. How would he know me? How does he know about what we're doing?"

"Maybe it's because of how well known you are."

I've been on a couple of major cases recently, and have gotten some notoriety for preventing terrorist attacks. That plus my amnesia history has made me a big story for the media to cover; I was their flavor of the month, at least for a couple of weeks. "It's possible, but I don't think so. Somehow he knows I'm on it."

"Maybe he waited around in the park to see the police response and saw you when you showed up. We need to get ahold of every picture taken there; he might be in one."

"Definitely. But Nate was there also, and he stands out somewhat more than I do. The Paterson cops were everywhere as well; Pete Stanton was in charge. It's also possible that the shooter knows me because of the investigation last time. I could even have come in contact with him."

We're coming up with a lot of possibilities, but that's all they are. Every one of them has to be followed all the way to the end, and each will take a hell of a lot of manpower.

The phone rings and it's Nate. He doesn't waste any time. "We got a hit on the silent alarm."

I know exactly what he means. Frank Muller, the guy who killed his wife in her Passaic apartment, has shown up in Englewood, at the house where they lived. We'd installed secret motion detectors and a silent alarm at the house, so that we would be tipped off if he came back to get some of his stuff. He had left everything there when he went on the run.

"Let's do it," I say.

There is no need for us to improvise here; we have a plan to put into effect for this eventuality. I ask Jessie to call in to the dispatcher to get it started, and I head for the Englewood house. Nate lives closer to it than I do, so he'll get there first, but he knows not to do anything until we're both there.

Nate and I are going to go in alone, at least until and unless we call in help. The area is a maze of houses and driveways, and under the cover of nighttime darkness, we don't want to spook Muller into taking off.

That doesn't mean the operation is just ours, though. Jessie's phone call will result in a blockade two blocks square around Muller's house. Air support in the form of helicopters with floodlights will be on call as well, but that's only if we lose him and he escapes into the adjacent area. But in that case it could be tough to find him regardless, which is why Nate and I want to make sure we nail him at the house.

Of course, it might not be Muller at all; it could be some kid trying to rifle the house, or maybe someone that Muller sent to get some stuff for him. If that's the case, then no harm, no foul, and we'll make any necessary arrest and head back home.

As I'm about to leave, Jessie gives me a hug and says, "Be careful."

"I will."

"And don't forget, this is the new you."

Jessie and Nate have frequently told me that the pre-amnesia Doug was a wild card, prone to take chances and not always worrying about personal safety. They say the post-amnesia me is more cautious and prudent, and they consider that a good thing.

I don't know either way, because I can't really remember meeting the old me. He sounds like he was more fun than the new me; someday I'd like to spend some time with him.

As planned, I park a block from the house. Nate's car is there, but he is not, which is annoying, but not entirely unexpected. He must have already gone ahead, probably to confirm that it's Muller, and to intervene if he tries to leave. We had left him that option, with the caveat that he doesn't reveal himself or try to take Muller down on his own.

There's nothing for me to do but head for the house myself. There's one obvious route from here, so maybe Nate will be waiting for me along the way. It's not an easy walk because it's a very cloudy night, meaning the moon is giving me nothing to cut through the darkness. The only light is coming from some rooms in a few of the houses, but that's barely enough for me not to bang into poles and dumpsters as I walk.

There's no sign of Nate as I go, and I'm starting to get worried. He can handle himself, but he shouldn't be trying to do anything like this on his own, if that's what he's doing. I draw my gun, so as to be ready for any eventuality.

It starts to rain lightly, which is of little significance except that it could make things a bit slippery if we're called on to run or make any sudden movements. Of course, that would be true for the bad guys as well as the good guys, so it's literally a wash.

I finally get within sight of the back of the house. There is one light on in a side room, which is a bit more than I could have hoped for. But it's still quite dark.

"Come join the party, dipshit!" It's a voice coming from the direction of the house, and it immediately triggers my worst fear. Nate had for some reason gone in first, and Muller had gotten the upper hand.

Within a few moments I see what I am dealing with; Muller and Nate have come into my line of sight. Nate is in front and Muller is directly behind him. He has a gun to Nate's head and is looking in my direction. He is also wearing night-vision goggles, something we had not anticipated and which no doubt allowed him to get the drop

48

on Nate. It explains how Muller could see both of us coming.

"Come on over here, asshole, and join your friend." When I don't move or respond, he says, "Now, or your partner won't have a head."

He obviously sees me, and I can't take a chance on him following through on his threat, so I step out into the open. I'm bathed in darkness, but with those night-vision goggles he's wearing, I might as well be sunning myself on the beach.

Once I've moved about ten paces toward him, he says "That's better."

I'm holding my gun with two hands in shooting position, aimed at his head. There is a very narrow window past Nate, maybe six inches. Nate is much taller than him, so his eyes are barely above Nate's shoulder. I will take the shot at the top of his head if I have to, but I wouldn't be confident about it, so hopefully I won't have to.

"Drop your gun," he says, causing me to speak for the first time.

"No fucking way," I say, since I am my most eloquent under pressure.

He doesn't seem impressed; in fact, he laughs. "Let me put it another way. Drop your gun or your partner goes down now."

"We have a situation," I say. "If you shoot

him, it will be the last move you ever make; that I can guarantee. If you try and shoot me, once you do he will grab your arm and break it like a twig. And then he'll follow up and do the same to every bone in your body."

Another laugh. "You think I care if I die? You think I would have come back here if I cared? I just want to take as many of you as I can with me. And I'm starting with this big piece of shit. So you've got three seconds to drop the damn gun, or I'll drop him."

This is a worst-case scenario; people who are quite happy to die are notoriously hard to intimidate.

"One."

I quickly go through my good options, which doesn't take long, because I don't have any. I could drop my gun, but that seems likely to get both of us killed; Muller has just announced that as his goal.

"Two."

I could take the shot; but it's a difficult one, made more so by the dim light. I could definitely miss, in which case Nate is dead for sure. Or I could even hit Nate; he's a pretty big target.

But I do believe that when he gets to "three," Nate is finished.

So I fire, and I blow off the top of the son

of a bitch's head.

I never did forget how to shoot.

"Holy shit," Nate says, as I walk toward him.

I've still got the gun pointed at Muller, though he is now lying facedown on the ground. His gun has fallen a few feet away, and I kick it to the side, but it's really not necessary. Muller is not making a comeback.

"Holy shit," Nate says again.

"You mentioned that already."

"You had about a three-inch window," Nate says.

"Turned out to be enough."

"You could have hit me."

I nod. "If it's any consolation, that would have ruined my night. Can you imagine the paperwork? And then the media would have been brutal. Headline would have been 'Fat Cop killed by Hero Cop.'"

Nate doesn't say anything. It takes a lot to shake him up, but this experience has done it. It would do it to anyone. My jokes aren't having any effect, and they haven't stopped my own legs from shaking.

"Nate, he was going to shoot you. I had to do it."

He nods. "I know and believe me, I'm fine with it. I can't believe you made that shot, under that pressure."

"No pressure," I say. "You were the one he was going to kill."

I don't bother asking Nate how he got into that position in the first place. I have no doubt that Muller set a trap for us, using his night-vision glasses, and that Nate walked into it first. It's probably better this way; had we gone in together he could have gotten the drop on both of us. Besides, the facts will all come out in the endless interviews that we are going to be put through.

Within a few more seconds the area is swarming with cops, all armed and ready for anything. The sound of my shot drew them in from the perimeter. No matter what had occurred, Muller wasn't getting out of here alive.

Officer-involved shootings result in a great deal of paperwork and post-incident analysis, and in this case officers were very involved. I am positive I acted correctly, and would do the same thing again. And I also am sure that there will be no negative repercussions.

Nate and I go down to the station to fill out our statements and sit for the first of the interviews. Captain Bradley is there waiting for us. "You have fun?" he asks.

"A blast," I say.

"Okay, tell them what they want to know, and then get back on your real job."

So we tell them everything, and it's past one in the morning before we are cleared to leave. Our cars have been brought to the station by other officers, and at least a dozen of them have waited around until the end of the interviews, in a show of support. These are gestures I very much appreciate, and I'm sure Nate does as well.

Nate and I walk to the cars, which are parked next to each other. As we reach them, Nate stops and says, "Doug . . . thanks. No kidding . . . thanks."

"Forget it, Nate. You would have done the same thing." Then, "But you would have missed."

He nods. "I would have missed intentionally."

Then he smiles. Welcome back, Nate.

Many cops go their whole careers without firing a shot in anger, and now I've killed four people in the line of duty. Two of them I remember; besides Muller I killed an organized crime figure who was involved in a terrorist plot. It's part of the reason I'm sort of famous today.

The other two I don't remember at all. Nate told me they were both guys who deserved it, and in both cases I apparently fired in self-defense and with good cause. I've gone back and read media reports of those incidents, as well as a lot of the internal reports that were generated by the department.

There is absolutely no indication that I did anything wrong, and the two guys that I shot were apparently total scumbags who had themselves committed murder. But even so, I took their lives, and it somehow seems weirdly disrespectful that I have no recollection of doing so.

Jessie has waited up for me; she is clearly well aware of what has gone down tonight. She greets me with a serious hug, which eases sort of naturally into a serious kiss. I've joked with Nate and acted nonchalant, but the events of the night have shaken me, and this is light years better than coming home to an empty house.

"This is the high point of my night so far," I say.

"I'm glad."

"Emphasis on the 'so far.' "

She smiles. "We'll see about that. First we

need to walk Bobo. I've been waiting to see if you were going to call. I didn't want to miss it."

So we walk Bobo. It's amazing; when I walk him by myself, he pulls me down the street like he's a horse and I'm a wagon. When Jessie walks him, he shuffles alongside her, matching her stride like they are the Rockettes. I have no idea how she does it.

Of course, in both cases I am left carrying the bag, literally. It's plastic, and its sole function is to pick up Bobo's shit. And believe me, Bobo can shit with the best of them. He could single-handedly fertilize Nebraska.

As we walk, I ask who she spoke to tonight.

"Captain Bradley. He called me as soon as it went down, just to say that you guys were okay. Then Nate called; I spoke to him a little while before you got home."

"I didn't have a choice," I say. "This wasn't the old me, or the new me. I had to do what I did; any me would have done it."

"He knows that, and he's grateful. He said the guy would have shot him in the head. He was about to try and take the guy down, but he doesn't think he could have done it without him pulling the trigger. He couldn't believe you made that shot."

"Let's not talk about it anymore, okay?" I ask.

"You're upset that you killed him?"

"Not even a little bit. I'm upset that I hesitated."

"What do you mean?" she asks.

"The asshole was counting to three. I let it go too far; I should have shot him on 'one.' "

She laughs. "Now that's the old you."

"Let's go back and get to the high point of the evening," I say.

"Yes. Let's."

Captain Bradley follows my advice and calls a press conference about the Randowsky killing.

Of course, the fact that it was my advice would have meant close to zero. That is because I gave the advice to Bradley, but by his own design he is not the decision maker. He is nothing if not careful, and he would have cleared this with the chief, the police commissioner, the mayor, the governor, and the emperor, if New Jersey had one.

There was a debate as to whether the commissioner, and even the mayor, should show up for this press conference. The commissioner wouldn't have spoken either way; Bradley is handling that solo. It was finally determined that if the commissioner and mayor were there, it would lend too much importance to the occasion. The powers that be want people to understand what is going on so that they'll be alert. But they don't want them to think that the situation is dire and worthy of panic.

Of course, I think that the main reason Bradley was given the whole show for himself is that this is the bad-news part. This is telling the public that the killer is on the loose. When the good-news part comes, when an arrest is made, there won't be a room big enough to hold all the brass looking to claim credit and bask in the glory.

So it's just Nate and me standing behind Bradley as he puts the message out. "Preliminary ballistics in the Alex Randowsky shooting," he says, "confirm that the weapon used is the same one that was used in the murder of Walter Brookings eighteen months ago.

"We are asking everyone with any information about either or both of these crimes to call and tell us what you know. You can do so anonymously, and a tip line has been set up that you can use. I urge you to do so."

Those are the basics, and once that is accomplished, Bradley says that he hopes everyone understands, but he will not be able to comment on the specifics of the investigation because it is ongoing and in the early stages.

He then opens the floor to questions, and the press comes up with about ten different ways to ask him questions about the investigation, forcing Bradley to say ten more times that he can't comment on the investigation, you know, because of the ongoing thing.

He does not mention the threatening note that I received. That would just cause greater alarm, without any benefit. It is also something that can be used to judge any possible future confessions; any legitimate confessor would have to be aware of the note.

I've got a hunch the actual killer isn't going to do any confessing.

Our first stop after the presser is to see Miriam Brookings, widow of Walter. She lives in a large house on Derrom Avenue in Paterson, which is coincidentally the street that abuts Eastside Park near the tennis courts. As a neighborhood, it is as close to ritzy as Paterson gets.

Nate had called Mrs. Brookings to alert her to what Bradley was going to say at the press conference, in effect giving her a heads-up that the wound that probably hadn't closed was about to be pried open even further. It was a considerate thing for Nate to do.

It's about twelve stone steps up from the street to the house; my guess is that UPS drivers would not look too favorably on this stop. I'm afraid I'm going to have to hire a crane to get Nate up to the top, but he makes it with surprising ease. Those fourteen ounces he's dropped on his four-year diet have really made the difference.

Mrs. Brookings has opened the door and is waiting for us at the top of the steps. "Hello, Nate . . . hello, Doug." There's a sadness in her voice, which is no surprise. What I focus on is the use of my first name; I obviously spent some time with this woman, who my memory tells me I have never seen before in my life.

Business as usual.

We go inside and she brings us our coffee, Nate's is with cream and artificial sweetener, mine just black. She didn't have to ask us how we take it, she just knew.

"How are you feeling?" she asks me. "I heard about your accident and have followed your heroism; I tell people I knew you when."

"I'm fine, thank you. It's good to see you again." I'm confident saying that; if she knew me when, then I must have known her when as well.

It's hard for me to make small talk, especially since it would probably be a repeat of something I've talked to her about in the past. But I see photos of two young children on the table, so I ask about them.

"Those are Walter's kids, but they are adults now. They'd been estranged from their father for a number of years. He loved them in his own way. I always thought that someday they would reconcile, but I also thought there would be more time. All of a sudden the time was up."

Now that I've established the kids as a conversational area that I should have avoided, Nate thankfully bails me out. "Did you watch the press conference?" he asks.

She shakes her head. "I'm sorry; I couldn't bring myself to turn it on."

"We understand. As I told you, the purpose was to announce that the killer is the same one as . . ."

He stops, reluctant to finish the sentence, so I pick up the ball. "The victim's name was Alex Randowsky; he was a local attorney. We're trying to determine if there was any connection between Mr. Randowsky and your husband."

She thinks for a while. "I don't believe I ever heard the name, but that doesn't necessarily mean that Walter didn't know him. Walter knew many people. We can check in his computer contact list."

She goes and gets her husband's laptop

and turns it on. "This hasn't been used in many months," she says.

A look through the contacts and an email search both turn up nothing. "I could check with the management people at the factory; maybe there's a business connection," she says.

"Please do," I say, and I give her my card.

"Do you have any idea who is doing this?" she asks.

I want to bullshit her, but I can't. "Not yet," I say. "But we will. And you'll be the first to know."

Steven Galloway is one of three founding members of the law firm Randowsky, Myers and Galloway.

He was playing tennis with his partner and friend in Eastside Park that day, a match which ended in that partner and friend taking a bullet in the heart.

Nate and I visit him in his office, which takes up one floor of a building in Ridgewood. We take the elevator to a reception area, but there is no receptionist behind the desk. In fact, there seem to be no people anywhere, and the lights are dimmed in here.

"Hello?" Nate calls out, and when there's no answer, he does it again.

"Sorry." It's a voice that sounds off in the distance, but a short while later a door opens and the owner of the voice is standing there. I assume it must be Steven Galloway, but he's not dressed in lawyer's clothes. He's wearing jeans and a pullover.

"We're closed," he says. "I gave everyone the week off; nobody felt like working because of what happened to Alex. I'm Steven Galloway."

We introduce ourselves and shake hands. "Thanks for speaking with us," I say.

"I told the Paterson police everything I know, which I'm sorry to say is absolutely nothing."

"Sometimes it helps to go over it again."

"Come on back to my office. I thought it might help to try and lose myself in work, but I was wrong about that. I can't concentrate on anything."

We follow him back, and as we pass a large office, he says, "That's Alex's office . . . that was Alex's office."

Once we're settled, Nate asks Galloway to take us through the events at the tennis court.

He nods. "We finished playing; we had played for a long time. It was a three-set match. Then we walked past courts one and two, behind the baselines because people were playing on them. We walked out together, then we said goodbye, because we were parked in different places.

"Then I heard this noise; I thought it might be a car backfiring — but then, cars don't backfire anymore, do they?"

Nate smiles. "I don't think so."

"Then I thought I heard someone scream, though not real loud, and I turned around. I don't think it was Alex who screamed. He was on the ground; it took me a while to realize what had happened. I thought he just fell or something, and then I saw all the blood. It was horrible. More people started to scream, and I'm afraid I was one of them. It seemed surreal, like it couldn't possibly be happening this way."

"Perfectly normal," Nate says. Then, "Did you see anyone do anything unusual? Maybe quickly get into a car and leave? Anything that, looking back, seems strange?"

He thinks for a few moments. "No. Not that I can recall. But if it was just someone leaving, I don't think there's any chance I would have noticed. I was pretty shook up."

"Can you think of any enemies that Alex might have had? Maybe because of issues involving work? Did he ever mention anyone he was worried about?"

"The Paterson cops asked me all of that, and I've been wracking my brain. Lawyering is an adversarial process, that can't be helped sometimes, but Alex was as well-liked as anyone I've ever met. I can't think of anyone he's gone up against, or the firm has gone up against, that could have done anything like this. Not in a million years."

"What about outside of work?" I ask.

He smiled. "For Alex there was no 'outside of work.' Work consumed him. The firm benefited from it, even if it didn't do much for his family life." Then, "Sometimes there's no room for both, as much as one might try." Then, "Starting now I'm going to try harder."

"What about any connections to Walter Brookings?" I ask. "Did Alex know him? Represent him? Go against him in court?"

Galloway's shake of the head is a firm one. "I know he didn't, because we talked about it when Brookings was killed. I knew Brookings; not well, I met him a few times. But Alex said he didn't know him personally. Of course he knew of him; Brookings was a prominent citizen."

We thank Galloway, ask him to call us if he thinks of anything, and leave.

I'm not surprised that we're not finding a connection between Randowsky and Brookings. If there is a link, I think it is only that they were both somehow connected to the killer. Everything runs through him.

Or maybe they were selected and targeted at random.

The truth is, we have no idea.

"It depends what we use as the metric," Jessie says.

She's addressing the team, updating all of us on what information she and her people have come up with. I know she'd rather be doing the listening than the talking, because that would mean she'd be going out on the street rather than sitting behind a computer.

But she's come to terms with it and has adjusted pretty well. And no matter how much it has bothered her, she never lets it affect her work . . . at least not that I can remember. The fact of the matter is that she is much more valuable in this role compared to being another one of us cops running down these leads, but I don't have nearly the guts to tell her that.

Maybe the old me had more courage; I don't remember.

The first topic of the session is the cryptic note sent to me that talked about the ninety-six "creeps" out of ninety-nine still on the wall. Since we only know of two killings, a major effort has been put forth to identify the possible third victim.

Jessie continues, regarding the metrics. "There are two basic things we can look for. The first is ballistics, whether the same M4 rifle was used in any additional shootings. We can safely rule that out, though we do have two shootings that utilized the same make and model of weapon. One is in the New York Metropolitan area, and information about both is provided in your folders. Of course, we have no way to be sure that the killer struck in this area, but I am sure you will want to prioritize geographically.

"The next metric is the method of killing, meaning one bullet shot directly through the heart. We also have a number of those, including two in this area. You have that information in your folders, and also included are single-bullet shootings that did not hit directly in the heart, but in relatively close proximity.

"There is no obvious connection between any of these victims to either Mr. Brookings or Mr. Randowsky, just as we are not aware of any connection between those two men themselves. But we are very early on here and haven't come close to running down all the possibilities. Obviously you'll also be doing that yourselves firsthand, out in the field."

She turns the floor over to Nate, probably because he's famous for using as few words as possible when speaking in any kind of public setting. "Thanks, Sergeant," he says. "Excellent work. People, we are going to run down every lead we have, and plenty that we don't yet have. Captain Bradley has authorized all the overtime we need, and vacations and days off are hereby considered nonexistent until we bring this son of a bitch down.

"Also in your folders are your specific responsibilities, so that there is no overlap. They will be updated daily, maybe even hourly. We have no time to make a false step; the note said 'three down,' which means there are likely more to come."

Left unsaid by Nate is the fact that forensics got absolutely nothing off the note — no print, no DNA, nothing. The envelope was sealed not with saliva, but with tap water.

None of this is surprising.

So now it becomes just a matter of legwork, hoping to uncover something that will solve the puzzle. Of course, we are more likely to catch a break than an inspiration, but we'll take either.

Looming over us is the knowledge that another victim could go down at any time. We don't know who to protect, other than ourselves. Our vests will fend off a bullet to the heart, though of course our shooter could always make an exception and center a shot in one of our foreheads.

Our first stop after the meeting is the Sunrise Senior Living Facility in Teaneck. In a shooting just five weeks ago, a woman by the name of Helen Mizell was shot while walking outside the complex toward a grocery store in a strip mall.

The seventy-one-year-old Ms. Mizell also received one bullet in the heart, but it was from a .38-caliber revolver. In addition to the location of the bullet, there are other similarities to the Randowsky and Brookings cases. The victim seemed to be targeted, though for no reason that seems apparent to anyone. No one saw the shooter, and no clues to the murder have been uncovered.

Sunrise Living is on four impeccably kept acres that feel like a college campus, without the Frisbees. Residents walk casually around the grounds, stopping to sit on benches and chat. It's the kind of place where I'd like to wind up when I'm at that age, and sometimes it feels like that will happen in about twenty minutes.

We've called ahead and are ushered in to see Joyce Peterson, the manager of the facility. She smiles a lot and offers us something to drink, which we decline. Once we bring up the Mizell shooting, her smile appropriately disappears.

"It is an ongoing nightmare," she says. "In addition to the obvious tragedy for Helen, it has had a terrible effect on our other residents. They are fearful, and I'm afraid they are correct in feeling that way."

"Tell us about Ms. Mizell," I say. We already know a lot about her from the investigative records that the Teaneck police provided us, but we tend to like to hear things ourselves.

"She was a bit younger than the average resident here, and was in good health. She had friends, but I'd say kept to herself more than most. She ate in her apartment fairly often, rather than the dining hall. But nothing terribly out of the ordinary.

"Probably the most social thing she did was play bridge; I don't play myself, so I have no personal knowledge, but everyone said she was a remarkable bridge player."

"Did she have many visitors?" Nate asks.

"No, I don't think so. If she did, they

72

didn't check in here as they are supposed to. But I'm not aware of any close family either. Someone said that she had two children, who I am told live in St. Louis. I'm quite certain that the police notified them, and our executive director did so as well."

"Did they come here when she was killed?"

"I don't believe so; I think her things are still in storage." Then, "Why would anyone have possibly wanted to shoot her? It just seems so bizarre, so horrible."

I know that the Teaneck police interviewed a number of the other residents, mostly members of Ms. Mizell's bridge group, but they had nothing to offer. It's not necessary for us to repeat those interviews; we'd wind up with even less than what we got from our talk with Mrs. Peterson, if that's possible.

Bottom line is I don't think her murder, bizarre and apparently inexplicable as the circumstances might be, is related to the Brookings and Randowsky murders.

Or maybe it is. When we catch the shooter I will ask him.

Danny Phelan has been identified as a priority by Jessie.

At this point that means he is above a pretty low bar, since we have no one close to being labeled a suspect. But Phelan has a number of factors on his record that make him very worth checking out.

For one thing, he has been in prison. He went in about a month after the Brookings killing and was released four months ago. We don't know when the apparent third murder took place, but it could easily have been within these last four months. The timing fits.

Another item which moves Phelan well up on our list is the fact that he is, or at least was, a gun collector. He was infantry in the army, which means he is quite possibly a proficient shooter. He also would probably be familiar with an M4.

Lastly, he was someone that I interviewed

after the Brookings murder, but I came to the conclusion that he was not our guy. I of course don't remember why I came to that conclusion, but my notes may explain it when I have a chance to go over them. I've only gone over the main files and was waiting to get to my individual notes.

This last factor leaves me with slightly mixed emotions. We need to nail down a suspect before he strikes again, but if I mistakenly let the killer walk last time, in my view it would make me responsible for the subsequent deaths. That would be tough to take.

Phelan had arrived in town not too long before the Brookings shooting — or, more accurately, he came back to town after some time on the run. He was surrendering himself to authorities on a drug warrant that went back a couple of years, and that's what he wound up serving time for. There are no reports of violence in his civilian record.

Based on Jessie's analysis, he seems like a good enough candidate that we've sent two officers out to his apartment in Elmwood Park to bring him down to the station. We want to put him under some stress, and that includes not giving him home field advantage.

When Phelan arrives he looks anxious and

more than a little angry. I hear him say "this is bullshit" to the cops that bring him into the interrogation room. Nate is watching through the one-way mirror; this is going to be just me, as it apparently was last time.

"What the hell do you guys want this time?" is his conversation starter.

"Hello, Danny, nice to see you again."

"Is this about Brookings again? Because that other guy got shot?"

"I just want to have a conversation."

"It is about Brookings, right? Well, no way; I'm not talking to you. Not without my lawyer. Maybe not even with my lawyer."

"You have something to hide?"

"My lawyer," he says. "I want him now."

"You can clear everything up right now without him; then you don't have to be bothered again."

"I know how you guys operate; you tried to put the Brookings thing on me. Now you're doing it again. I'm not saying a word."

"You're making a mistake, Phelan."

"It won't be the first. Are you arresting me? If not, I'm out of here."

I try some more to convince him to talk to me, but I get nowhere. This guy has been through this before and is not about to let himself get trapped. So I send him on his way, at the same time moving him to the top of a very short suspect list.

Once he's gone, I dig in to everything we know about him, as contained in the file and in my notes.

The reason I questioned him back at the time of the Brookings killing was that his car was parked illegally near where the shooter was judged to have fired from. The car had gotten a parking ticket, so we knew for certain that it was there.

He claimed that his car was stolen and later recovered. It seemed like a bullshit story, even though he had notified his insurance company about the theft, but I apparently couldn't nail him on it.

His lawyer is a local attorney named Andy Carpenter, who is known as something of a hotshot in Jersey legal circles. He's had some major victories in high-profile cases and is not exactly worshipped by the cops he's cross-examined.

I would have said that I've never met Carpenter, but according to my notes, I talked to him about Phelan back during the investigation. It was shortly after that conversation that I made the determination that Phelan was likely not responsible for the Brookings shooting.

I've got a sick feeling in my stomach that

I might have made a mistake. If I did, Randowsky and an unknown third person are dead because of me.

With maybe more to follow.

"I am nothing if not patient," the shooter thought.

In fact, it was even a source of pride, of professionalism. To rush, to preempt the natural flow, was to invite a problem, to open the door to a mistake. Better to follow the plan, to let everything unfold naturally, and to take advantage of the perfect moment. Breathe normally, be relaxed and comfortable.

Then fire.

You only get one shot at a target. The shooter knew that, and therefore knew that the circumstances needed to be just right. But that wasn't really a problem because everything had been planned out, and missing was not an option.

The shooter felt that it reminded him of what they always said about lawyers, which was never ask a question you don't know the answer to. In his world, he changed that to never shoot at a target you aren't positive you will hit.

And sometimes the opportunity did not present itself, at least not in a completely satisfactory way. Better not to take the shot and wait for next time. There would be no harm in letting the victim live for another day, or two, or three.

Of course, with the note already sent, that would be slightly embarrassing. On the plus side it would sow more confusion, and the shooter smiled at the prospect.

But on this day the opportunity would come, his patience would be rewarded. Chuck Maglie's day at his place of employment, the Marriott in Saddle Brook just off Route 80, had come to an end. Chuck was a bellman and, when called upon, doubled as a valet parking attendant.

He had been there for three years and was a valued employee, which meant he was reliable. He showed up for work every day and did what he was supposed to do. After all this time his personnel file did not include a single complaint from a hotel guest, which in the hotel world was remarkable.

It was a Tuesday, so not very busy. Not many people checked in or out on Tuesdays, so Chuck didn't have that much to do. He didn't like that because it also meant he earned very little in tips, but it did make for an easy day.

Chuck's shift ended at six o'clock, as long as his replacement showed up. The guy's name was Vinnie, and he could be counted on to be there on time. That wasn't true of the last guy who had the job, but he had gotten canned and Vinnie was brought in.

In Chuck's mind, Vinnie's arrival hadn't necessarily been a change for the better. Chuck didn't mind working overtime; he had nowhere in particular to go and he could use the extra money.

Chuck lived in a one-bedroom apartment in Lyndhurst, and when his work ended all he generally did was go home, cook himself some dinner, and maybe go out to the corner bar for a drink. If that process started an hour or two later because he was needed at work, so be it.

When Vinnie arrived that night, Chuck brought him up to date on everything he needed to know. For example, he told Vinnie that the guy in 218 wanted his bags brought down at 6:30, and would need his car brought around as well. Then Chuck went out the back door, like he always did, because at the far end of the rear parking lot is where employees parked their cars.

Chuck was reaching for his keys when the

single bullet hit him in the chest and sent him flying backwards into a Subaru Impreza.

This is not my first time at Charlie's sports bar in Paterson.

I'm not really much of a sports bar kind of guy. I'm a big fan of the New York teams, mainly the Giants, Knicks, Mets, and Rangers, and they're all on the television stations we get at home. Jessie's a big fan as well — actually much more intense about it than I am, so we watch a lot together. Doing so gives our den sort of a sports bar feel, because she screams at the TV a lot.

But I've been to Charlie's a couple of times and I like it. The food is right up my alley: terrific wings, burgers, and fries. So I wasn't too upset when Pete Stanton told me to come by, that I could find Andy Carpenter here.

Apparently Pete and Andy hang out here quite a bit, evidence of an unlikely police officer–defense attorney friendship. And sure enough, when I arrive I see them sitting at a table with another guy I recognize as Vince Sanders, editor of the local newspaper.

I wasn't counting on Sanders being here, and I have no intention of talking in front of him, but I'll let the situation play out.

"Hey, here he is," Pete says, when he sees me. "That evens it out. Two upstanding men of the law, and two dregs of society."

I say hello to all three of them, though Sanders is able to pull off a handshake without taking his eyes off the TV showing the Mets game. It's late in the season, and the Mets have already effectively been eliminated from postseason action, so I'm not sure why he's so intense about it. Maybe he's betting the game.

"What are you eating and drinking?" Pete asks. "Andy's buying, so price is no object."

I know that Carpenter is very wealthy. I think I heard that he had a big inheritance, and he's certainly had some lucrative cases. "I'm not having anything," I say. "I just want to talk to Andy."

"Now that is refreshing," Andy says. "What about?"

I know Pete already told him the purpose of my coming here, but apparently Andy wants to hear it from me.

So does Sanders. "Is this on the record?"

he asks, ever the newspaperman. He asks the question while still staring at the television.

Andy points to a table across the room. "You are going to spend the next fifteen minutes over there. . . ."

Sanders interrupts. "No way. This is my table."

"You didn't let me finish," Andy says. "The rest of my sentence was 'or that is the last beer of yours that I am ever going to pay for.' "

"You can't intimidate me," Sanders says. "But just the fact that you tried pisses me off so much that I am going to sit over there." With that, he picks up his beer and goes off to the table Andy had pointed to.

Andy points to Pete. "Now if I could only get rid of this guy that easily." Then, "What's on your mind?"

"Danny Phelan."

"You mean the Danny Phelan you tried to browbeat into talking without his lawyer present this afternoon? That Danny Phelan? The one who paid his debt to society and wants to live without fear of police harassment? That Danny Phelan?"

" 'Browbeat' is not the word I would use. I wouldn't go with 'harassment' either."

"Seems to fit," he says. "In any event, we

already had this conversation a couple of years ago."

"There have been more shootings. The hiatus seems to fit neatly with the time that Phelan was away."

"I'll tell you what I told you last time," he says. "Danny is a lot of things; he's not a murderer. The only wounds he causes are self-inflicted."

I know from my notes that Carpenter took on Phelan as a client because his accountant, Sam Willis, is Phelan's cousin. The representation was originally just to facilitate Phelan's turning himself in on the drug charge, and hopefully to keep his sentence as short as possible.

"So bring him in and tell us where he was when the shootings took place," I say. "Give us a reason not to suspect him."

"Look, Danny Phelan screwed up a good part of his life. He took drugs, and then he sold them to pay for the ones he took. But he's admitted it, and he came back and made good on it. He lost his family, or at least part of it, but he got his life back. He's a smart guy, and he's a good guy, and he is not a guy that gets off on hiding behind some rock or tree and shooting people. You can keep going after him, but you're wasting your time."

"Is that what you told me last time?"

I can see the look on his face as he realizes what happened. "Right. That amnesia thing. That must be a pain in the ass."

"I manage."

"Yeah," Andy says. "That's what I told you last time. He'll cooperate, but I need to be there. I would just suggest you not waste your time; this is not your guy."

Pete pretty much snorts up his beer when he hears this. "Doug, the guy is a defense attorney. Take everything he says with a grain of horseshit."

My phone rings, and I see that it's Nate calling. "Yeah?"

"Where are you?" Nate asks.

"About to head home."

"That ain't happening," he says.

"Why not?"

"We got another one."

I stand up, but before I leave I turn to Carpenter. "We're going to need to know where your boy was tonight."

The Marriott is one of a string of hotels lining route 80.

Route 80 is an amazing road. You can get on it in Teaneck, not far from the George Washington Bridge, and drive all the way to San Francisco. You never have to leave the highway, unless of course you want to eat, or sleep, or go to the bathroom. That's where these hotels come in.

Route 80 is the main reason these places are here, since it's not as if cities like Hackensack and Paterson are tourist hotspots. They literally tower over the area, and are clean, comfortable, and self-contained, with gyms, pools, restaurants, and room service. If you want to be near New York without paying New York prices, they represent a decent alternative.

And tonight this particular hotel, the Saddle Brook Marriott, has something that they won't feature on their website: a dead body and blood spattered all over the back entrance.

By the time we arrive the word has made its way to the Saddle Brook police that the state police are in charge. I'm sure they had no desire to resist the directive, and would be aware that they have no power to do so anyway. So basically they have just locked down the scene until our arrival.

The goal of the first arriving cops in this type of situation, which is usually brief, is similar to physicians . . . "first, do no harm." They want to secure the scene, make sure the criminal event is concluded and there is no more danger, keep onlookers away, and insure no evidence is tampered with.

It's not necessarily an easy job. For just one example, they don't want to walk around and tromp on potential evidence in the area where the killing took place, but they do need to examine the victim in case he or she might still be alive.

The parking lot is crowded when we arrive, but a large area around the body has been cordoned off. An ambulance is already there, but there is no one to rush to the hospital. The coroner's van will be more functional, but it has not arrived yet.

One media truck is here, no doubt soon to be joined by many friends. Since these shootings are taking place so close to New York City, it has become a huge story, and getting bigger all the time. Within minutes there will be a caravan of media trucks arriving, and a few minutes after that reporters will be breathlessly talking, with the hotel in the background over their shoulders.

Nate shows his identification to the local cop in charge, but there's really not a lot for us to do until our forensics people arrive. I do tell the cop to instruct his people to take photographs of the onlookers; there is always a chance that the perpetrator hung around to watch the police react to his handiwork. It wouldn't be the first time.

There's unfortunately not much for us to see and certainly no surprises. The victim, who has been identified as a bellman named Chuck Maglie, has one noticeable wound from a bullet that entered his chest in the area of his heart.

We don't need a coroner to tell us the cause of death, or whether Maglie died instantly. And we don't need Sherlock Holmes to tell us that this is related to the other killings.

The hotel manager tells me that he has a man in his office named Anthony Young, who seems to have been the only witness to the shooting. Nate stays near the victim so that he can direct forensics when they arrive, and I head off to question Mr. Young.

Young is obviously shook up. He's sitting alone in the manager's office, leaning forward in his chair. He looks up when he sees me. "Is he dead? What am I asking . . . he's got to be dead. Of course he's dead."

I don't see any reason to lie, so I confirm the fatality. Then, "Where were you at the time of the shooting?"

"There were no parking spots near the main entrance in front, so I was driving around looking for one. I was checking into the hotel, so I figured if I found a spot close enough, I'd park and walk with my bag around to the front.

"As I was passing near the back door, I saw a guy come out in a bellman's uniform. I thought maybe he was working and would take my bags, but that wasn't going to work because I couldn't find a space close enough.

"So I was going back to the front to leave my bag, check in, and then find a place to park. Just as I was going to turn, I saw the bellman guy fall backwards and go down. At first I thought he slipped or something, and then I figured maybe he had a heart attack. So I jumped out of the car to help him, and that's when I saw the blood. God, it was awful."

"Did you hear anything unusual?" I ask.

"You mean like a shot?"

"Anything."

"No, I don't think so. But I still had the window closed, and I listen to satellite radio."

"Do you play the radio loud?"

"No, not really." Then he gives a slight grin of embarrassment. "I listen to show tunes; nobody plays show tunes really loud."

"You said he fell backwards. Can you describe that?"

He thinks for a moment. "He just took like half a step back; I'm not even sure if he moved his feet. It wasn't far or anything; he wasn't blown backwards like you see in the movies. It was like he was slightly jolted, almost pushed, but his legs went out from under him and he dropped."

We'll know for sure when forensics gets to do their work, but my guess is the impact of the bullet was lessened by the distance that it traveled. Add in the fact that the sound of the shot was not loud enough to be heard over the satellite radio, and it's clear that our shooter was probably a good distance away, but not enough to make him miss.

Our shooter doesn't miss.

I get Mr. Young's contact information and tell him he's free to go, but that we might be wanting to talk with him again. He says that he's going to be driving for a while and then checking into a different hotel. I can't say that I blame him; most people in his situation would get in the car and drive to San Francisco.

By the time I get back outside, the scene is being fully processed. Captain Bradley has arrived as well, not a great surprise considering the developing importance of the situation.

"Anything to go on?" Bradley asks me, referring to my interview.

"Not yet. Next mistake our boy makes will be the first."

He nods. "A bellman. Hard to figure."

I know what he means. The first two victims, at least the ones we know about, were a successful businessman and a prominent attorney. On some level it could have been an attack on elite society, but killing the bellman rebuts that theory.

"Still could be someone getting revenge on people he has a grudge against. We'll check potential suspects as we get them against hotel records. Who the hell knows? Maybe he stayed here and the bellman mishandled his luggage."

"Speaking of potential suspects, you got any?" Bradley asks.

"Maybe one."

"Phelan? Nate tells me you're back to thinking he's a possibility."

"That's all he is right now. But he knows we're looking right at him. If he did this today, he's rubbing our noses in it."

I got nothing out of the brief talk with Andy Carpenter.

It was disappointing. I wasn't expecting anything incriminating; the guy is smart and he's Phelan's lawyer. What I was selfishly hoping for was some information that would actually exonerate Phelan, that would demonstrate that he is not our guy.

But that didn't happen, and it didn't happen back at the time of the Brookings shooting either. Phelan still remains a suspect, in fact, our only viable one, though that is a pretty low bar. But as long as there is a chance he is the killer, it remains possible that I let the killer go back then.

The implications of that to me, in light of subsequent events, are obvious and awful. I want to catch the killer, and I want to do it quickly, but I do not want his name to be Danny Phelan.

Our ballistics people identify the location

from where the shot was fired. It's a secluded area near the back of the parking
lot; it slopes upward, which would have
given an unobstructed path for the shot.
They say that the shooter could easily have
taken it from inside his car, and certainly
there are no shell casings or other pieces of
evidence that can help us.

If we're waiting for the shooter to make a
mistake, we could be waiting awhile.

By the time I get home it's almost mid-
night and Jessie has waited up for me. She
doesn't even bother to say hello, she just
says, "You got another note."

"Here at the house?"

She nods. "I went out to get the mail a
few minutes ago, and it was there."

"Did you open it?"

She doesn't answer, instead just frowns at
me. It would be unprofessional and incom-
petent for her to have opened it, and she's
annoyed that I would think her capable of
that.

Oops.

It's on the dining room table, already
placed by Jessie in one of those plastic gallon kitchen bags to protect it. A bunch of
postal employees have obviously touched it,
and it's been through some postal machines,
but protocol is to treat it as if it's evidence

gold, and that's what Jessie has done.

I look at the envelope through the plastic, and it seems similar to the first one. I can pretty much predict what it will say, but it will be up to forensics to examine it and tell me. In any event, it can wait until morning.

But even without an examination, the note already tells me two things, the first of which Jessie verbalizes. "This was mailed yesterday," she says. "If it relates to the hotel shooting, he knew what he was going to do, and when he was going to do it."

"Our boy is a planner," I say. "And he's confident. He knew he would get it done."

It's up to me to say the other important thing that this note tells us. "He knows where we live."

"Yes, that much is clear."

My mind immediately starts mentally scanning our neighborhood, to think if there are any places a shooter can take a position at very long range and hit us in front of the house, or even through a window. I can't think of any; the houses in this area are pretty close together. But I'm far from sure of it.

"Starting now you need to wear a vest," I say. "He's playing with me, and taking a shot at you could be part of his fun and games."

"You don't have to convince me," she says. Then, "You think it could be Phelan?"

"Probably not, but I certainly don't have any better ideas."

"So what's next?"

"I'll bring this note in tomorrow morning, have it analyzed, and come up with nothing. Then I'll go over the reports filed by every damn cop in the department, all of whom are working on this, and come up with nothing. Then I'll look through the forensics on the hotel shooting, and come up with nothing."

"What then?"

"And then I'll put some more pressure on Phelan while I wait for the next shooting."

"Sounds like a fun day," she says.

Before we go to bed, I put the note up on a shelf for the night. I'm afraid that if Bobo should get hungry during the night and decide to eat the table, he might inadvertently eat the note as well. "The dog ate my evidence" excuse would be unlikely to go over well with Captain Bradley.

The last thing I do is pull the drapes closed.

Just in case.

Cynthia Morris is Danny Phelan's ex-wife. This is apparently not something she is eager to advertise, since she has dropped the name Phelan, though she had used it for the duration of their eight-year marriage.

But just because she doesn't want to use his name, that doesn't mean she wants to avoid talking about him. On the contrary, when Nate set up this interview, she seemed very eager to do so. Nate's guess, based on her response, was that she would not spend her time with us praising her ex.

Ms. Morris lives on Twenty-Fourth Street in Paterson. The houses are well-kept, but no one is going to confuse the neighborhood with Beverly Hills. It's populated by hardworking people who unfortunately usually have to live paycheck to paycheck.

Even though we are in plain clothes and driving an unmarked car, a number of residents standing outside give us the stare as we arrive. They don't seem angry or resentful; it's more that our arrival is an interesting development in an otherwise dull day.

I don't think any of them doubts who we are; my guess is Ms. Morris told them we were coming. We are local celebrity-makers.

She's on the porch waiting for us as we walk toward her house. She's a heavyset woman, probably fifty years old, wearing a dress that I would imagine is not her normal hanging-around-the-house outfit. She's also wearing a good amount of makeup, which may or may not be her typical procedure.

All we're doing is stopping by to conduct an interview with her, but she prepared like she's going to the prom. Had I known I would have brought a corsage.

"You're right on time," she says, maybe thinking we are craving her approval. "Come on in."

We introduce ourselves and thank her for seeing us, and she asks if we want any coffee. Nate accepts the offer and I don't, and she says that she thinks she has some Oreos to go with it. I think Nate may ask her to marry him.

She comes back with a cup of coffee and an open box of Oreos, placing both down on the table in front of Nate. He shows admirable restraint, waiting almost five seconds before attacking the package.

"Ms. Morris, as Detective Alvarez told you, we would like to talk to you about your husband."

"Ex-husband," is her quick correction.

"Sorry. Ex-husband. When were you divorced?"

"Not soon enough," she says.

"Can you be more specific?" I'm doing most of the questioning, since Nate's mouth is pretty much full of Oreos.

"He left about twelve years ago, but he came back once in a while and tried to get me to give him more chances. I did a couple of times, but I'm not that stupid, you know? We were officially divorced about two years ago, not long before he went to prison."

"He had some drug issues?" I ask.

She laughs. "Yeah, he had plenty of issues. I mean, I can take care of myself, and I was glad to get rid of him. But he had a daughter who loved him; she still does. Don't ask me why, 'cause I sure as hell don't know."

"Have you been reading about the shootings, or seeing the coverage on television?" I ask. There's no way to ask her the questions we need to without her finding out why we're asking.

She nods. "Yeah, I heard about them."

101

Then she actually brightens. "Is that what this is about?"

If Phelan were shown to be the killer, she would get the pleasure of his going down while at the same time assuming the role of biggest celebrity in the neighborhood. She'd have hit the daily double.

"I'm sorry, but the way this works is that we need to ask the questions. It's policy; when we can inform you of certain things, we will."

"Okay," she says, obviously not happy with the policy.

"Are you personally familiar with any of the victims? I'm specifically referring to Walter Brookings, Alex Randowsky, and Chuck, or Charles, Maglie?"

"You mean did I know them?" she asks, but doesn't wait for an answer. "No, I never met them."

"What about Danny? Are you aware as to whether or not he knew any of them?"

She thinks for a moment, trying to figure out how to implicate Phelan. "I don't know for sure, but Danny knew a lot of people. I'll bet he knew the men you're talking about."

"Did Danny keep guns in the house?"

"Are you kidding? He could have fought a war with them."

"Did he take them with him?" I ask.

"You're darn right. I didn't want those things in my house for another second."

"We're going to send some people around with a photograph of a rifle. We'll want to know if you recognize it."

"OK," she says. "Whatever I can do to help."

"When was the last time you saw Danny?"

"Like I said, a couple of years. Just before he went to jail. I saw him with Julie on the street."

"Who's Julie?"

"My daughter. His daughter. They're big buddies now," she says, with obvious disapproval. "She visited him in prison a bunch of times, although she tried to keep it from me."

"We'd like to talk with her. Does she live here?"

She shakes her head. "She lives with her boyfriend; she thinks he's going to marry her. She might be right, 'cause he gave her a ring. Julie and I got tired of fighting about her asshole father. She just has a blind spot about him."

"We'd like to talk to her," Nate says, having swallowed enough of the cookies so that he can get a word out.

Ms. Morris again completely ignores the

103

issue; she's not finished bad-mouthing her ex-husband. "He gives her nothing her whole life, but she calls him 'Daddy.' She visits him in prison, brings him stuff. Can you believe that?"

"We'd like to talk to her," Nate says, once again.

"I mean he's Mr. Perfect Father until she's fourteen, then he starts doing drugs, and he has no time for her. So he takes off, making me mother and father. Who does that?"

This is clearly a woman who has family issues; it's time for me to jump in. "Ms. Morris, we understand what you have gone through, but we need to talk to your daughter."

"So talk to her. What do I care? Just don't believe anything she says about her father."

She finally gives us Julie's contact information. We thank her, Nate grabs two more Oreos, and we leave.

We're no sooner in the car than Jessie calls. "We've got a live one," she says.

"How so?"

"Guy by the name of William Gero. He bought an M4 two years ago, and he's a marksman; believe it or not, he owns a shooting range."

"That's it?"

"Of course that's not it," she says. "Shows

104

a tendency toward violence. Two arrests for assault, though in both cases the charges were dropped. That's the only reason he still has a gun license."

"Why were they dropped?"

"Arresting officers think he threatened the victims, but they couldn't make it stick. One of the victims was his ex-wife."

"And that's it?"

"You going to keep asking that?" she says. "When we get to the point where that's it, I will so inform you."

I laugh. "Yes, ma'am."

"There's one other thing," Jessie says. "The reason that woman was Gero's ex-wife was that she divorced him. And when she divorced him, she was represented by none other than Alex Randowsky. And Mr. Randowsky reported after the fact that Gero threatened him."

"Okay," I say.

"Now that's it," she says.

The River Edge rifle and pistol club is, not surprisingly, in River Edge.

I've been to a couple of clubs like it, mostly for shooting contests, but never this one. It's an upscale place, as befitting its location, which means that a good percentage of its clients are weekend shooters who enjoy pretending to be Roy Rogers. They also want to be able to protect their family at home, though if they ever have to use their guns, their families would be wise to take cover.

There is an indoor and outdoor range, though the outdoor range cannot be seen from the street or the parking lot. But we can certainly hear the shots being fired as we pull into the nearly full lot. I would imagine that much of the clientele wants to get their outdoor practice in before winter hits.

We're here to see the owner and proprietor, William Gero, and because of the nature of our visit, we're a little wary. By definition, our talking to Gero at this location means that he is armed.

We head for the main desk. There's a receptionist sitting there and a guy behind her doing something with a large glass case containing a bunch of weapons. I assume they are for show and not for rent to members; firearms are not bowling shoes.

The receptionist asks if she can help us, so I show her my badge and say, "We'd like to talk to William Gero. Is he around?"

The guy behind her whirls around, leaving no doubt that he is, in fact, Gero. "I'm Bill Gero," he says. "What can I do for you?"

I introduce Nate and myself and identify us as state police detectives. "Where can we talk?" I ask.

He frowns to the point that it morphs into a moan. "Oh, come on. Is this about Randowsky? I told a friend of mine that I bet you'd come around."

"The question was, where can we talk?" Nate says.

"What about right here?" Gero says, in effect challenging Nate, which in my experience is not usually a great idea.

"What about at the station?" Nate says. "Let's go."

Gero raises his hand in a quick surrender. "Okay. My office is private. We can go in there."

For a second I think Nate is going to drag the guy to the station by his collar, which we have no reason to want to do. Instead he nods, and we follow Gero back into his office.

Once we're seated, Nate says, "Tell us about Alex Randowsky."

"You know more about him than I do. He was a lawyer, he was a scumbag, and now he's dead."

"You threatened him."

He shakes his head. "I didn't threaten him. I called him a piece of shit and a few other stronger names, all of which were accurate. But I didn't threaten him, and I sure as hell didn't kill him."

"What did you have against him?" I ask.

"He represented my ex-wife, and he got her to lie through her teeth. But hell, that was three years ago. You think I waited three years to take a shot at him?"

"Where were you the night before last at six thirty?"

"Night before last? You mean that hotel thing? You think I'm a goddamn serial killer? I think I need my lawyer here."

Nate picks up the phone on the desk and

hands it to Gero. "Call him and tell him to meet us at the station in fifteen minutes."

Gero thinks for a moment and then says, "I'm not going to pay that son of a bitch's hourly rate. Night before last at six thirty, I was here. Going over the books."

"Anybody with you?"

"No. We close at six."

"Do you have an M4?" I ask.

"Is that what they used?"

"That answer is not exactly right on point."

He nods. "Yeah, I have one. You probably know about it already because I bought it legally."

"What do you use it for?"

He shrugs. "Target shooting. Right here at the club. Everything aboveboard."

"So it's here right now?" I ask.

"Yeah. This is where I shoot it . . . legally."

"Can we take it with us to check it out?"

"No way. I don't trust you guys. No offense."

I smile. "None taken." Then I turn to Nate. "Maybe you should call for a warrant. We can all sit here until it comes through." Then, back to Gero, "It'll take a couple of hours, but we're not walking out of here without the rifle."

It's an empty threat; we don't have nearly

enough on Gero to get a warrant. All we have are suspicions, and suspicions don't usually carry much weight with judges.

But empty threats often work; that's why we make them.

"Yeah, you can take the damn rifle," Gero says. "But you'd better bring it back."

"And then a bellman happened to fall. Ninety-five creeps left on the wall."

Sergeant Tony Arguello, who works in forensics, has brought Nate and me copies of the note that was mailed to me at the house. There's no reason for us to see the original; since it's evidence, we wouldn't be able to touch it anyway.

"You get anything off of it?" Nate asks.

Arguello shakes his head. "No prints, no DNA, no nothing."

"And no surprise," I say. "Any way to tell where it was mailed from?"

"It went through the Englewood post office, but we have no way of knowing which box it was dropped in."

"What about the paper and ink?"

"Bic pen and the kind of computer paper you can buy in a ream at a supermarket," he says. "This guy is not the type to make stupid mistakes."

"Which is probably why this won't come to anything," I say. I hand the rifle case that we got from Gero to Arguello. "There's an M4 in there; test it to see if it matches our boy."

"Wow . . . you think there's a chance?"

"No," I say. "But test it anyway."

Once he leaves, I call to arrange for a patrolman to take some photographs of an M4 out to Danny Phelan's ex-wife to see if she recognizes it as something that he owned. It's a long shot, but that's all we seem to have to deal with.

The internal phone rings and I pick it up. It's the desk sergeant, who says, "There's a woman out here wanting to see you."

"Me?"

"Yeah. She says she's Danny Phelan's daughter."

"Send her in."

I quickly let my mind go through all that I've learned about Julie Phelan from the files and from her mother. She is twenty-four years old, and even though her father abandoned her and her mother when she was fourteen, she has remained an ardent supporter of his.

She was a frequent visitor of his in prison; the prison records show that she was the only visitor Danny Phelan ever had. So it's rather likely that she is here to tell us that he is totally, completely, and absolutely innocent.

"Hi," she says, when she walks in. She seems a bit shy and almost reluctant to step in the office.

I introduce Nate and myself to her, offer her a soda or water, and ask her to sit down. She asks for a bottle of water and takes a big gulp of it before launching into the reason she's here.

"My mother told me that you came to talk to her about my Dad."

Nate nods. "We did. We were going to come talk to you as well, but you beat us to it. So thank you for that."

"She doesn't understand him," Julie says. "He's a good person, and all he wants is a second chance. She wouldn't give him that chance, and he's better off without her."

"That's what you came to tell us?" I ask.

"Yes, and to say that it is ridiculous that you think he might have shot those people. My father would never hurt anyone, except himself. But that is all behind him."

Nate asks her specifically if she has ever heard her father mention Brookings, or Randowsky, or Maglie. It does not come as a shock to us when she says that she has not.

"But I can tell you this," she continues. "The newspaper said that the man at the hotel was shot the night before last at six thirty in the evening."

"So?"

"So I was with my dad. I brought over some heroes and we ate them at his apartment. We watched a baseball game."

If she's telling the truth, we just lost our leading suspect. But we've also just eased my potentially guilty conscience.

The shooting of Chuck Maglie has shaken the public far more than the previous ones.

I'm sure that part of it is just because it comes so soon on the heels of the Randowsky shooting. Brookings and Randowsky were many months apart, and people didn't really feel the connection, even though we announced it. But now, with Maglie following just days later, it's starting to feel like a state of siege has taken over.

Also, I think on some level Maglie's occupation contributes to the panic. Brookings was a very successful businessman and Randowsky a prominent attorney, so it felt like if there was a pattern, it was that elites were under attack. But Maglie was a bellman, a common working man, so his death broadens the range of those who have legitimate reason to be fearful.

Bradley is about to start another press conference, which Nate and I are stuck attending. This time the mood is a bit more contentious; based on what I've been reading in the newspaper and seeing on television, the press is hungrier for information. Nobody is going to meekly accept the "ongoing investigation" excuse for avoiding answering the tough questions.

This time, unlike the first press conference, the chief, commissioner, and the mayor are all here. I'm sure they don't want to be, but my assumption is that they made a value judgment.

On the one hand, they certainly don't want to stand here and say they don't have a clue who is killing their citizens. It makes them look impotent and ineffectual. In the mayor's case, "Impotent and Ineffectual" does not make for a good election campaign bumper sticker.

But the offset is that not to have shown up would send a signal that they don't give a shit about those same citizens.

Clearly they have opted for appearing to give a shit.

Bradley starts off by thanking everyone for being here. He says that he will provide a brief update on the investigation and then the mayor will say a few words. Then they will take questions, though Bradley once again cautions that he knows everyone will understand that he can't get into details of the "ongoing investigation."

"I'm going to be very up-front and direct," is how Bradley starts, and I think I see the mayor wince at the words. "We now have three shooting victims: Mr. Brookings some eighteen months ago, Mr. Randowsky, and Mr. Maglie this week. I assume you all know the circumstances and locations of these shootings, since you've reported on them extensively."

He goes on to say that our collective hearts and prayers go out to the victims and their families. I've got a feeling that's not going to be sufficient either to placate the families or solve the crimes.

Bradley continues, "All three of these gentlemen were shot with the same weapon, an M4 rifle. We are therefore operating under the assumption that there is one perpetrator, and that perpetrator is an accomplished marksman.

"I am telling you these details because we need the help of the public. If you know someone who possesses this type of weapon, and also has a demonstrated ability in marksmanship, then we want that person's name.

"But I want to be careful not to limit it to that. If anyone has any information that might be of help to us, no matter how vague it might be, we want to hear from you. There is an anonymous tip line set up; just call, tell us what you know, and we'll take it from there. Every little bit of credible information helps, no matter how small.

"We have a number of persons of interest, but no one that has risen to the level of suspect, and therefore no one we are prepared to name now. I understand the concern of the public, I share it, and I can only assure you that every resource we have is dedicated to putting this killer behind bars. And with your help, we will do just that."

Bradley turns it over to the mayor, who sets a mayoral record for fewest words spoken at a press conference. Then he steps way back . . . so far back that I'm afraid he'll fall off the makeshift stage, in order to leave Bradley to answer questions on his own.

Bradley takes a half-dozen questions, but no one succeeds in getting any more information out of him, and the truth is, he has no more information to give. When it ends, as he is leaving, he whispers to me, "I don't want to go through this again. Catch the son of a bitch."

When we get back to the station we are greeted with the unwelcome news that the ballistics tests on William Gero's M4 show that it is not the rifle used in the shootings. I'm not surprised, though I am disappointed.

This doesn't clear Gero entirely; he could certainly have another M4 that we don't know about. This is a guy who owns a rifle range. The unknown other weapon might have been purchased illegally, making it a more likely candidate to be used in the commission of a crime.

Gero has the closest thing we have to a motive, at least in the Randowsky shooting. The guy represented his ex-wife in a contentious divorce. But if there was a category below "person of interest" — maybe "person barely on the radar screen," then that's where Gero would be stationed.

I see on my desk that there is a message to call Andy Carpenter, Phelan's attorney. I call him back, and he says, "You wanted to know where my client was the night of the hotel shooting."

"I still do."

"He was having dinner at Patsy's."

I know Patsy's; it's an Italian restaurant in downtown Paterson known for its great pizza. "Who was he eating with?" I ask.

"Two of his friends," Carpenter says, and gives me their names and phone numbers.

"What time?"

"They got there at seven fifteen. The reservation was in his name."

"Where was he before that?" I ask. The shooting was at 6:30, so this does not get Phelan off the hook.

"He was home, and then drove to the restaurant. He didn't stop off to lie in wait and shoot a bellman."

"So says his lawyer."

"So says his lawyer about his innocent client," Carpenter says. "I'm telling you, you're wasting your time. And if you charge him, I'll get him off, and you'll have wasted more time."

"I may want to talk to him again. Tell him not to do any traveling."

"We'll come in whenever you want. We are concerned citizens, dedicated to helping our police avoid the public humiliation of arresting the wrong person and then having to issue a less-than-heartfelt apology."

I get off the call. The alibi that Carpenter provided is not conclusive, but that's not what I'm focusing on. Julie Phelan told us that she brought in hero sandwiches that night, and she and her father watched a baseball game.

Now I find out that forty-five minutes after the shooting, Danny Phelan was at

Patsy's with a couple of his friends. My guess is that the story will check out.

What all this means is that Julie Phelan lied.

"She was covering for her father," Jessie says. "She believes in him, and she stupidly made up a story to help his situation. She thought you'd buy it and leave him alone."

"She lied to law enforcement, which is a crime in itself," I say. "I know that because I happen to be law enforcement. I could show you my badge, and I know the secret law-enforcement handshake."

"So what are you going to do?"

"I don't know. Nate is pissed about it; he thinks we should charge her, or at least scare the hell out of her. I'm a little less worked up about it. What do you think?"

"I think you should keep your eye on the ball; this is just a daughter stupidly trying to help her father. In the grand scheme of things it's not important. Does Phelan's restaurant alibi hold up?"

I shrug. "Yes and no, but more on the no side. He was definitely at Patsy's, but he would have had time to do the shooting and then go to the restaurant. So it's not really an alibi at all."

"So he's still your best bet at this point?"

"I'm afraid so," I say.

"Why do you put it that way?"

I'm not sure I want to go where this conversation is going, but I go there anyway. "Couple of reasons. First of all, if Phelan is our leading candidate, it means we don't have much in the way of candidates. Because even though we have more on him than on anyone else, it doesn't mean we have a hell of a lot on him.

"And second, if by some chance he's the shooter, it means I missed him last time. Which means that Randowsky and Maglie and someone else died because of my miss. And there's still a lot of potential victims left on that wall."

"It happens all the time, Doug. We have a suspect, and then we back off, and then we go after him again. An investigation is a fluid thing; you can't get it right the first time every time."

"I'll remember that," I say. "It will be one of the few things about the investigation that I'll remember."

"Don't start feeling sorry for yourself," she says.

"Thanks for the advice. I'll try and remember that too. Maybe I should be taking notes."

I may not be the brightest bulb in the socket, but I know when I'm being obnoxious. Rather than trying to correct it, it's easier to exit the conversation, which is what I do by taking Bobo for a walk. Bobo is even less likely to put up with my shit than Jessie.

We walk into town and stop at a small deli. I sometimes get Bobo a bagel as a peace offering. He takes the entire bagel in his mouth in what seems like one gulp; it's a scary sight. When he's finished, he just looks at me in disgust, as if to say, "That's all you got?"

The town seems less crowded than usual. I heard someone say on the radio that people in North Jersey have been less inclined to leave their houses because of the shootings. I don't know if this is evidence of it or not; it's possible it's just an off night in town.

When I get home I sit down to go over the case files that I've brought home with me. We have so many cops working the case that I don't have nearly enough time to read all the reports they file during the day.

The first one is some background stuff on the hotel shooting. There are a bunch of witness reports, which are basically mis-named, since only one person actually witnessed anything. But there is one of some interest to me. A woman who had parked her car near where the shot was fired reported seeing a white SUV parked at a strange angle.

The woman noticed it when she retrieved her car at least a half hour before the murder took place. In fact, she was halfway to Pennsylvania before she even heard about the killing on the radio.

It triggers something in my mind, but I'm not at all sure if I'm right. "You feel like taking a ride?" I ask Jessie.

"Where to?"

"Garfield."

"I hear Garfield is beautiful this time of year," she says.

"Think of it as my way of making it up to you for being so obnoxious before."

"I don't think Garfield will do it, but it's a first step," she says as she grabs the car keys.

I program Phelan's address in the GPS, and we're off. Twenty minutes later we pull up to his house.

I know it's his, because of the address, and because there is a Ford Escape in the driveway. It's an SUV, and it's white.

"You shouldn't come over for a while," Danny Phelan said. "The police are trying to pin these shootings on me."

His daughter Julie had come to see him, which in itself was not unusual. It was rare that a week went by without her at least talking to him, and that included the time he was in prison. But this time she had brought along her fiancé, James McKinney.

Danny had met James a few times; he didn't know him well at all, but was pleased that James had made Julie's life easier financially. That's something he was never able to manage.

"I know," Julie said. "I spoke to them."

"They came to your house?"

"No, I went to see them. The cop named Brock and his partner. A big guy."

Phelan turned back to Julie. "Why did you do that?" He was clearly agitated at hearing this.

Before she could answer, he turned to Mc-Kinney. "You need to stop her from doing these things."

McKinney smiled. "Believe me, I have tried. Your daughter has a mind of her own."

"Mom told me they suspected you, so I wanted to tell them they were wrong, that you would never do something like that."

"Your mother spoke to them also?"

She nodded. "Yeah. I figured she didn't have such good things to say. She never does, so I wanted to set them straight."

"You got that right about her." Then, "Thanks for doing that, honey, but you should stay out of it."

"There's just one problem: I lied to them."

"How?"

"I told them that the night the guy at the hotel got shot, I brought in heroes and we watched television."

"Why did you say that?"

"I thought if they knew you couldn't have done that one, then they would leave you alone on all of them. There's no way they could know I wasn't here, right?"

Phelan knew this was a problem. He had told Andy Carpenter that he was at Patsy's that night, and Carpenter would have told the cops. They'd know that Julie was lying, and they would think he might have put her

127

up to it. Either way, they might come down hard on her for it.

"Julie, don't lie to them anymore, okay? If they talk to you, tell them the truth."

"You think they know I lied?"

He nodded. "Yes. You don't know anything bad about me, right?"

"Right."

"Then there's no reason to lie. I can take care of myself."

"Okay. If you say so."

"I say so." Then, "How come you never asked me if I was involved, you know, in what's going on?"

"Because I know you're not."

He thought she was going to add, "are you?" but she didn't. "Good. That's my little girl."

"I'm not your little girl anymore. I used to be, before you left. But now I'm not."

"I know."

"Dad, why don't you let James help you? He has money, and he said he'd help you get started in some kind of business."

James and Phelan really had never had a chance to establish any kind of relationship, but James had made the offer to help before, no doubt as a favor more to Julie than to him. "Thank you, James, but I don't need any help. I'll be fine. You can take care of Julie."

"I can take care of myself, Dad. We have that in common."

As Julie and James were preparing to leave, Julie said, "Give me a minute to talk to my dad alone, okay?"

James seemed fine with that and said, "Of course. I'll be in the car."

Once he was gone, she said, "Dad, we want to help in any way we can."

"Thank you, honey. But I'm fine."

"If you need to go someplace, for however long, James has a cabin you could use. It is in the middle of nowhere, north of here, in the woods, and it is in his brother's name, so there is no reason anyone would ever find you there if you didn't want to be found."

Suddenly Danny was interested. "Maybe at some point I'll take you up on that, depending on circumstances."

"Good. It's just sitting there unused. We wouldn't tell anyone where you were."

Once Julie left, Danny had time to think of the implications of the fact that the police had questioned Cynthia, his ex-wife. They hadn't sought out Julie, but they no doubt would have if she hadn't gone to them.

With all they had going on, the fact that they had found the time to conduct those two interviews meant that he was a key suspect in their eyes. If that was the case already, he knew that pressure would only increase once they found out more. And he knew they would find out much more.

Cynthia was a major problem. If she hadn't already, she would tell them about his guns, and the fact that he had taken them from the house, even though as a felon he was prohibited from having them. Worse yet, she would tell them about the M4.

It was getting close to the time when he would have to disappear. At least now he knew where he could go.

"Of course I interviewed him. I interview every driver I hire."

The interviewer that I'm talking to is Evan Meyer, who runs Meyer Trucking. It's based in Clifton, and I've come to his office because this particular person that he interviewed is Danny Phelan. And after that, he hired him.

Meyer is going out of his way to show me how busy he is, to the point where he's reading through papers on his desk while we're talking.

"He was a driver for you?"

"Yes. I have a trucking company, and trucks need drivers."

He's still reading papers on his desk, which is getting on my nerves. My nerves are pretty easy to get on these days. "Those papers must be really important if you have to read them while we're talking," I say.

He looks up at me. "I've got a business to

run. I'm in here at six o'clock in the morning, and I leave at eight o'clock at night, which means I have no life. All I have is this business. And once an employee leaves, I no longer give a shit about him. Okay?"

I smile. "No problem. While you're running the business and reading those important papers, I'll just call some friends of mine. Maybe you know them; they also are busy. They get in early, and they leave late. And what they do in the hours in between is check on trucks and buildings to make sure they are completely up to code, just for safety purposes."

"Are you threatening me?" he asks.

"Not a chance. You want to talk, or you want to read?"

He thinks about his options for a moment, and then pushes the papers to the side of his desk. "I'll talk."

"Good. When you hired Phelan, were you aware that he was a convicted felon, on drug charges?"

"Yeah. He told me. But he was clean; we drug test all our drivers. And he's a veteran; we only hire veterans."

"Are you a veteran?" I ask.

"Damn straight."

"How many days of the week does he work?"

"Now?" he asks. "None. He quit two weeks ago."

"Did he say why?"

"No. Didn't say anything. Just stopped showing up. Never even picked up his last check."

I stand up and give him my card. "If you hear from him, I want to know about it." Then, "You can go back to your reading now."

The note was in my mailbox when I got home from work.

This time I didn't wait for morning; I brought it right down to the station to be examined. Once again I didn't open it, and I touched it as little as possible.

We've been through this often enough that I don't expect we will find anything, but that doesn't matter. Evidence is evidence, and there are ways to handle it.

I call Nate and together we stand over Sergeant Ferrara in the forensics department as she opens the letter, having already confirmed that there are no useful prints on the outside of the envelope.

She uses instruments to open it, then unfolds the note using the same instruments, which is basically a fancy, expensive pair of tweezers. She's going to be examining the note carefully for DNA and prints, but first she allows us to read what it contains.

Written in the same block letters, no doubt in ink from the same pen, it says:

HAVE YOU FIGURED OUT WHO ELSE FELL OFF THE WALL YET? I'LL GIVE YOU A TINY HINT . . . THE BITCH'S NAME WAS HELEN MIZELL.

I know that Nate has to be as stunned by this message as I am, but we leave without saying so, and we head straight for Captain Bradley's office. On the off chance that he's still here, we might as well have the conversation in front of him; no sense talking about it twice.

I'm surprised to see that he is, in fact, still here; these are unusual times, even for a police captain. He ushers us right in; as detectives in charge of this investigation, we have priority status.

"Doug just got another note," Nate says. "The victim we couldn't identify is Helen Mizell."

I know that Bradley has been keeping up with the filed reports as much as he can, but I can tell by his face that he's drawing a blank on Helen Mizell. "I give up; who is Helen Mizell?"

"She's a woman that lived in a senior-living facility; Nate and I were over there and talked to the director. She was killed with one bullet near the heart, but it was a thirty-eight."

He nods. "I remember now; I read the report. Shit."

"Right. Now we have no common thread among the victims; they appear to be random. And we have no common weapon."

"But we do have the one shot through the heart," Bradley says.

"For now. If he's willing to change the weapon, he could change the method. But I doubt it; he seems to like his safe distance."

"If it was a thirty-eight, it wasn't that long a distance. No matter how good he is."

Nate says, "There could be other victims we don't even know about. They could even be in other states; we cross-checked them all on the ballistics. Now that's out the window."

"I don't think so," I say. "Our boy seems more than eager to claim credit. He was even afraid we'd miss this one, so he gave us the name. If he had any other conquests, I think he'd be rubbing our noses in it."

"How carefully did you look into the Mizell killing?" Bradley asks.

I shrug. "Not very. We were just covering

136

our bases. Like I said, we talked to the director of the place, but not to the other residents. The local cops had done that, and turned up nothing. The victim wasn't even on the grounds when the shooting happened. She was walking into town."

"You want to send someone out there to conduct interviews?"

"No, we'll go. We'll talk to everyone, and we'll turn up the same nothing the local cops did."

"For the moment I don't want to go public with this," Bradley says. "At least not now. We don't want to scare every old person in the state. If I thought it would reduce the danger, I would. People are already afraid to go out of their houses."

I agree with the decision, at least for the time being, and I say so, as does Nate.

Bradley adds, "And who knows, maybe our boy didn't do it, but is just claiming credit."

"No chance," I say.

Bradley nods. "Yeah, I know."

On the way out to the senior home, Nate says, "Listen, pal, much as I'd like to trade up when it comes to partners, I think you should take some precautions. Our boy seems preoccupied with you; it's one small step from there to adding you to his list."

"I don't think so. Communicating with me is part of his fun."

"He can switch to a different kind of fun just like he switched to a different weapon. All I'm saying is change your patterns."

"How so?"

"Like don't walk Jessie's horse-dog around the neighborhood. Like keep your drapes closed. Like walk to the garage from the back of the house instead of the front. You're a cop; you figure it out. Just do it."

"I'll think about it."

"You'll think about it?" Nate asks. "You sure you want to make that big a commitment?"

"I'm sure."

We arrive at the retirement community and surprise the director, Joyce Peterson, who didn't expect to see us again. I can tell that's the case because she says, "I didn't expect to see you again."

"Just covering all our bases," Nate says. "We'd like to talk to Helen Mizell's closest friends, if they're still here." I'm just relieved that Nate said, "if they're still here," rather than "as long as they haven't died of old age yet."

"Well, as I told you, she mostly kept to herself, but maybe you'd like to speak to her bridge partners?" Peterson asked.

I nod. "That would be good."

So we spend most of the next two hours talking to Helen Mizell's bridge partners, during which time we find out that she was an excellent bridge player.

Now we're making progress.

"Did you tell them about the guns?" Julie asked.

Her mother nodded. "Damn right I did. And they sent someone around with a picture of a rifle, and I said Danny sure as hell had one of those, even though I can't tell one from the other."

"I'll tell them that you're lying."

"That's Daddy's little girl," she says, mocking. "The only problem is, even though I hate the son of a bitch, I don't really think he's going around murdering people."

"You're back to attacking him," Julie said. "I think that's funny."

"What's so funny about it?"

"Because while he was here, you couldn't stand him, you made his life miserable. Then he left us, he left me and you, and all you did was want him back. Now he comes back, but not to you, and you hate him again. Make up your mind, Mom."

Cynthia didn't want to argue; she was tired of arguing. "It's complicated," she said.

"That's always your fallback, Mom. It's complicated. Well, you know what? It's not that complicated. You're either for him or against him. You're either for me or against me. Black and white. It's pretty easy when you boil it down to that."

"I was always there for you," she says.

That draws a laugh from Julie. "Yeah, right. Well, I can see we're into the bullshit portion of our conversation."

"Don't talk to me like that."

"Why? Are you going to send me to my room? Goodbye, Mom."

"Julie . . . ," she said, but there was no use finishing the sentence, because Julie had already slammed the door behind her.

There was nothing terribly unusual about the argument between Julie and Cynthia; Cynthia could remember countless conversations that had gone in the same direction, and ended the same way. This one was no different, nor would the next one be.

It had all started when Danny walked out on them; nothing had ever been the same after that.

So Cynthia did what she always did in situations like this; she put it behind her and just went about her business.

"We've got another victim, and the world has officially changed," Nate says.

"What do you mean? Who is it?"

"Cynthia Morris, Danny Phelan's ex-wife. Bullet through the heart as she walked to her mailbox."

I let the news sink in for a few moments, then say, "Well, that's that."

"I'm heading to the scene now," Nate says. "Meet me there?"

"No. All we're going to find is a dead woman lying in front of a mailbox with a hole in her chest. We can do that later. Right now we need to bring Phelan in."

Nate agrees, and we immediately call in a team to cordon off the block where Phelan lives, with another group of cops to be with us when we go in and get him. Technically right now we're just bringing him in for questioning, but if we have to we'll make it an official arrest. Either way, once we get our hands on him, we are not letting go.

Once those arrangements are made, I call Bradley and update him on our plan, which he endorses. Then I briefly consider whether I should call Andy Carpenter once the cordon is established and give him the option of convincing his client to surrender peacefully. I decide against it. He'll just tell me that we have the wrong guy, that when the murder was taking place, Phelan was delivering Meals on Wheels to the elderly.

Bradley arranges for a warrant from a judge, just in case Phelan doesn't welcome us into the house. It will only delay us a few minutes, I have no doubt that once the judge knows which case we're working on, he is not about to jerk around with us.

It's getting dark, which in this case is probably a good thing, in that it will be harder for Phelan to see what is going on and track our movements. By the time Nate and I get there, the cordon is established, and the sergeant in charge assures us that no one has left that house or gotten through the barriers that have been set up on the streets.

Nate and I, along with four heavily armed SWAT cops, plan to approach the house from various angles. But there are no lights on in the house; either Phelan has kept them off because he knows we're coming, or he's not home.

We have devices which can measure heat sources within a structure; don't ask me how they work, I just know they do. The SWAT team has them as part of their everyday equipment, and in this case they tell us that there is no human heat coming out of that house at all.

If Phelan is in there, he's dead.

We take all of our normal precautions regardless as we approach the house, just in case the heat-finding machine is giving a false negative. I don't want my headstone to read, "He wouldn't be here if the damn heat-detecting machine had worked."

It's not necessary for us to break down the front door because it's unlocked. And sure enough, Phelan is nowhere to be found. I have a hunch he's not just taking in a movie.

I'm glad we have the warrant because it gives us the opportunity to take the place apart and look for anything that might possibly implicate him in these killings, or tell us where he might be.

Tellingly, there is no computer, smartphone, or tablet to be found. Unless he is a resident of the dark ages, he took them with him. I also don't see any suitcases, and drawers are emptied. This guy is not coming back.

Now I do call Andy Carpenter. "Your client's ex-wife just got herself a bullet in the heart," I say. "Talk about your coincidences."

"Damn," is his response.

"Do you know where Phelan is? He seems to have evacuated his premises in something of a hurry."

"No idea," he says. "But there's an obvious, innocent explanation for all this."

"What might that be?"

"Beats the shit out of me. But there is one."

"My suggestion is you get him to turn himself in."

"Thanks for sharing that, Lieutenant. I'll take it under advisement."

Meanwhile Nate is on the phone with Bradley, suggesting an all-points bulletin be put out for Phelan. I have no doubt that Bradley will be all too delighted to do it, and to let the public know about it, since he has to announce another murder at the same time.

I'm not sure if Bradley will publicly designate Phelan a "suspect" or a "person of interest." My guess is the latter. The public response will be just as significant, and if by some miracle it turns out that Phelan is not the killer, the department will not have as much egg on its face as if it called Phelan a suspect, only to be proven wrong.

I'm a little uncomfortable that we don't have any concrete evidence of Phelan's guilt, though if he has truly run, then that is certainly a significant factor. Also, Cynthia Morris's killing had not been reported by the media at the point that her ex-husband had taken off — only next of kin would have been notified — so if that is what precipitated his doing so, then he had to have independent knowledge of it.

Firing the shot is a foolproof way to get independent knowledge of a shooting.

Nate and I are not necessarily the best choices to run an investigation like this.

This role is very much about managing the army of cops at our disposal, reading their reports, directing their movements, and connecting the dots. But Nate and I like to be out in the field, which puts us temperamentally at odds with our assignment.

So for the time being at least, we're doing what we apparently did back when the original Brookings investigation was underway. We split up, with one of us out in the field and the other back at the station, pretending to be the boss. It's a good compromise between what we want to do and what we have to do.

Today it's Nate's turn to stay back, which is why I am going to talk to Julie Phelan. I would talk to her anyway, but now it's even more important, since a neighbor commented that Julie was seen leaving her mother's house about fifteen minutes before the shooting.

I am surprised when I see where Julie lives; it's in a fashionable neighborhood in Montclair. The house is owned by James McKinney, and one way or the other, he has clearly managed to give Julie an economic advantage that her parents never did.

I had called in advance and spoken to McKinney. I asked about his relationship to Julie, and he described himself as her fiancé. When I told him I was coming over, he said that Julie was very upset about her mother's death. If that was meant to dissuade me, it didn't work, because here I am.

McKinney opens the door for me as I approach and lets me in. We walk into the den, and he says, "Julie's in her room. She's pretty upset."

I guess he thought the "Julie is upset" approach would be more effective in person than it was over the phone. "Understandable," I say. "I won't take up much of her time."

He nods and leaves the room, hopefully to get her. When he comes back he says that she's getting herself together and will be down in a little while. Then he mentions again how upset she is.

The delay in her arrival unfortunately gives us ten long minutes to make small talk, which is among the kinds of talks I have no interest in. But he tries, talking about the Giants football season and the weather.

I think I'm supposed to keep up my end, so I ask him what he does for a living, and he tells me he's a broker.

I've actually got a fairly large amount of money, at least for me, because in the time after I was recognized as a hero for stopping a terrorist attack, and before I came back to the force, organizations paid me to do motivational speaking.

I'm not sure how much motivating I did; most of the audience looked like they were having trouble keeping awake. But they paid me ridiculously well and seemed quite content to do it. It embarrassed me, but I was basically pleased to take the money.

In any event, I'm not going to mention any of this to McKinney, since it is possible his broker's eyes would light up. Instead I ask him, "How long have you and Julie been together?" That's more than just small talk; it's a way of trying to gauge how much he knows about Julie's family, including her father.

He smiles. "Depends on when you start

the clock. We met at camp; she was at a girl's camp, and I was at the boy's camp next door. We were there for one year each, but we had a fling." Another smile. "We snuck back and forth a lot, but we were fourteen, so I'm afraid it wasn't close to a full-fledged fling. Then we didn't see each other for years, but we reconnected a couple of years ago. Picked up where we left off."

Julie finally comes out, looking like she's been crying and holding a crumpled-up tissue in her hand. A mother getting shot and a father occupying the position of key suspect in her murder and others will do that to a child.

"I've been telling Lieutenant Brock about our time at summer camp." James smiles when he says it, no doubt trying to lighten the mood.

She's clearly not into mood lightening, so she just stares at him without responding. Then she turns to me and manages a hello and sits down across from me, in effect giving me the floor. "I'm sorry about your mother," I say.

She nods. "Thank you."

That out of the way, and since this is a multiple-murder investigation and not a pity party, I let her have it. "You lied to me."

"What? No —"

"Yes, you did. You told me that you spent the night of the murder at the hotel eating heroes with your father and watching a baseball game."

"I did."

"Who was playing?" I ask.

"I don't . . . the Mets."

"The Mets were off that day," I say, having no idea if that's true. "And your father ate dinner at Patsy's."

McKinney jumps in, trying to avert a disaster. "Lieutenant Brock —"

"I'm not talking to you," I say. "So please don't interrupt. If you do, Julie and I will conduct this interview at the station, alone."

I turn back to Julie. "Now, we were discussing the time you lied to me. Which, by the way, is against the law."

She nods, hiding behind some tissue dabbing. "I just didn't want you to think my father could have done these things."

"Okay. From now on, let's stick with the truth. When was the last time you saw your mother?" I ask this knowing that she was seen leaving that house not long before the shooting.

"Yesterday. A short while before she was shot."

"What did you talk about?"

"My father. We argued about him, just like

152

always. She hated him."

"Did he hate her as well?"

"He didn't really care about her either way. He was over that a long time ago." Then, "And he didn't kill her."

"Do you know where he was at the time?"

"No."

"Do you know where he is now?" I ask.

"Why? Is he missing?"

"Let's go with my question. Do you know where he is?"

"No."

"Let me know if you find out. You'd be doing him a favor."

I leave, not knowing whether or not Julie actually knows where her father is. But she's lied to me before, so I have no reason to think she wouldn't do so again.

I call in and make arrangements to get a judge's permission to place a tap on Julie's phones. If Phelan calls her, I want to learn what they say and, hopefully, where he is.

Scott Holman, like most people in the Metropolitan area, watched Captain Bradley's press conference.

He hadn't watched the previous ones because he had been working, but he was certainly aware of the shootings and had even been going out less frequently, just to be cautious.

There had been a story in the paper about how local restaurants have been suffering, because many people had also decided it was just more prudent to be at home. Holman had no trouble believing that.

Holman lived in Leonia and worked in Manhattan doing corporate publicity. He had his own small, boutique agency, which meant he could make his own hours and work from home as often as he liked. He was at home this particular day because he wanted to focus on another project apart from his job. And with his wife out and his kids in school, he could do so without much interruption.

Holman was one of three people on his high school reunion committee. His was the Englewood high school class of 1994, so it was the twenty-fifth reunion. It was the first one the class had ever had, so it had taken months to gather as much contact information as they could on their former classmates, so as to contact and invite them.

Holman had taken on the responsibility of putting it all together. It was a huge job, much more than he anticipated, but he had finally gotten a handle on it. This day would pretty much put on the finishing touches. The RSVPs had come flooding in, and now he would go through them and find out who was coming, as well as whether they wanted the chicken or the fish.

But he stopped what he was doing to watch the press conference. He listened as the police captain welcomed the assembled press, thanked them for coming, and said that he had a couple of announcements to make.

He briefly summarized the killings that everyone already knew about, but then said that the investigation had uncovered another murder that could be attributed to the same perpetrator. It was then that he stunned

155

Holman.

The photograph they showed on the screen was Helen Mizell, who had been one of Holman's teachers at Englewood High. She taught English, and Holman remembered that she was known as "Hollerin' Helen," a term that came about because she was exactly the opposite of that description. She spoke so softly that the only people in the class who could hear her were those in the front. Since no one had any particular desire to hear her, the front seats always filled last.

In fact, all these years later Holman remembered his first day in her class. Not knowing about her soft way of talking, he had taken a seat in back. When she first spoke, he turned to a friend named Tom Ireland, who was sitting next to him in the last row.

Holman said, "I can't hear her back here," and Ireland had responded, "That's the beauty of it."

As Holman remembered it, he only had her for one class. He had no particular feeling about her either way, neither liked nor disliked her, possibly because he couldn't hear her. Other than that it was an unmemorable class and a nonexistent teacher-student relationship, but it still seemed weird and disconcerting to have this connection to a murder.

If Holman thought that was a shock, he was about to experience an earthquake. Captain Bradley followed this up with some news that the public had been desperate to hear. They had a "person of interest" in the killings. He was careful not to label that person a suspect, but certainly that was the impression he left.

The announced person of interest was Daniel (Danny) Phelan. They put up a photo of Phelan, which Holman recognized immediately. It had been almost twenty-five years since he had last seen Phelan, back in the days when they were both in the same class at Englewood High.

Holman had heard something about Phelan being in prison, and, in fact, had not been able to get any contact information to invite him to the reunion. But seeing his photo like this, and hearing that the police clearly considered him a candidate to be the serial killer, was beyond stunning.

The fact that Helen Mizell had been killed and Danny Phelan was the possible killer was way off the coincidence charts. Bradley said that they did not know where Phelan was, and he gave the tip line number for any and all information.

But what the hell could he have had against Helen Mizell? Had she done something to him twenty-five years ago that drove him to kill her? How could that be possible? He strained to remember some incident that might have happened, but could come up with nothing.

For all Holman knew, the police were aware of the high school connection already. But he still felt that he should call and point it out, just in case they did not know.

So he picked up the phone, and as he did, he knew one thing for certain: Danny Phelan would not be having either the chicken or the fish.

Danny Phelan seems to have dropped off the face of the Earth.

Ten minutes does not go by without a tip coming in from a citizen swearing that they have seen him. Phelan is either eating at the diner, or sitting on a park bench, or taking in a movie, or riding a bus, according to these people. Unfortunately the next tip to pan out will be the first.

It's only been three days, which is not that long a time, but it feels longer. What worries me the most is Phelan's infantry experience; more specifically, the training he would have had that could facilitate his apparent disappearance.

It's why I am in Manhattan meeting with General Willard Thielen in his hotel room. The general is in town to give a speech at an American Legion event, and the army has offered him up as a gesture of cooperation with our governor, who did the asking. The fact that the governor was himself a former general certainly would have facilitated the cooperation.

General Thielen is a decorated combat veteran. He's approaching sixty now, but he's got the body of a forty-year-old, and the eyes of someone considerably younger than that. I consider myself reasonably tough, but I'd much rather be meeting him in a hotel room than a dark alley.

At our request, Thielen has reviewed Phelan's service record, and prefaces his comments with the caveat that he is not personally familiar with Phelan and only knows what he has read.

"I understand that," I say. "But he's a fugitive, so I need to understand his capabilities."

"They are considerable," Thielen says. "You already know he's a marksman."

"Unfortunately, yes. Tell me more about his training."

"Well, certainly he is well trained in the combat skills, hand-to-hand and otherwise. His proficiency scores are about average, but we are talking about a group of people with very high skill levels in these areas. His was a very special unit. He also had considerable survivalist training."

I nod. "Which means he has a significant

ability to remain concealed?"

He thinks for a moment. "Here in an urban environment like this? Probably not much better than anyone else. I see no evidence that he is a master of disguise, if that's what you mean."

"And elsewhere?"

"Put him in the deep woods and he could outlive us all. By definition he's been trained to survive by living off the land. If he's somewhere like that, and he doesn't choose to come out, it would take battalions to find him."

"And if he comes out, it will probably be to shoot people."

"I sympathize," Thielen says.

"Is there anything else in his record that would help us?"

"Well, are you aware that he did not leave the service voluntarily?"

"He was dishonorably discharged?"

"No, that was avoided. He had some incidents; one was drug related and the other two were assaults while off base. In situations like that, it is frequently suggested to the soldier that he find other employment."

I nod. "He wound up having drug issues that eventually put him in prison."

"That is no surprise."

"Thank you, General. One last thing: Would you have a record of the people he served with? In his units?"

"I could get it easily, with one phone call. What is it you want?"

"I want to know if Walter Brookings or Alex Randowsky turns up anywhere in there." I write out the names for him to refer to.

"I can certainly find that out. Shall I call you at your office?"

"Yes, please," I say, and I give him my number. Then I thank him and leave. When I get in the car, the traffic report tells me that the George Washington Bridge is backed up and the Lincoln Tunnel is the better way to go.

So I decide to go through the tunnel, but apparently everyone else had also listened to the report, so it takes me an hour to get through.

By the time I get to the station, the general has delivered, and there's a message that he has the information and I should call him back. It's impressive, but I guess when you're a general you can do impressive stuff.

Once he's on the phone, he's short and to the point. Walter Brookings served in the same basic training unit as Danny Phelan. Randowsky's name is nowhere to be found.

So Brookings and Phelan served together and therefore obviously knew each other. What a coincidence.

Richard Decker always joked that he should be the mayor.

He'd lived almost his entire life, all thirty-eight years of it, in Sussex, New Jersey. The only exception was the time he spent in college, brief though it was. Decker had gone to Fordham, on its beautiful campus called Rose Hill, incongruously tucked into the Bronx.

It turned out that academics really weren't Decker's thing, and he only lasted two years before he and the university agreed that they were not a good fit. His time in college was not covered in academic glory, but he had a damn good time.

But the reason that Decker jokingly aspired to be mayor of Sussex is that it was originally called Deckertown when it came into existence in 1891. It was named after its founder, Peter Decker.

Richard could find no evidence that he

was related to Peter Decker, even eagerly buying one of those retail DNA kits to make the connection. That didn't work out so well for his main goal, though it did connect him with a previously unknown second cousin.

So the non-mayor had been dutifully and successfully working away at his service station near the intersection of Routes 23 and 284. In terms of traffic it was not exactly the West Side Highway, but since everyone in town patronized the place, there was more than enough business for him to make a good living.

Tuesdays were not particularly busy days for Richard, so he usually manned the station by himself. He had the townspeople coming by in normal fashion, but not too many transients came through. People traveling, those going camping, usually started and ended their trips on weekends.

Richard was inside the station, changing the tires on Roger McFarland's car. Roger was an old friend; they grew up together. And he was a great customer. Roger was on the road all the time as a salesman, so he changed tires about as often as most people change socks.

Richard heard the sound of a car pulling up, and he looked out and saw Betty Mc-Cain. New Jersey is the only state in America that doesn't allow people to pump their own gas, but in Betty's case it wouldn't matter. Betty was not the gas-pumping type.

So Richard walked out to pump the gas, as well as clean her windshield and check under the hood. He believed in providing the best service at all times, even though he was the only game in town. In fact, that may have been one of the reasons he remained the only game in town.

Richard liked to make small talk with his customers, particularly the locals, but in Betty's case that was pretty tough. She had no interest in sports, and he knew from town meetings that they were on opposite sides politically. She was said to be an outstanding weaver, but Richard didn't have too many weaving anecdotes to share.

That left the old standby, weather, and Richard figured the crisp fall air would be a good place to start the chat. But he never got a chance to mention it. One step out of the station and he was set back by the force of the bullet. He was dead long before he hit the ground.

"Brookings and Phelan were in the same army unit together," I say.

Nate has just gotten back from some time in the field conducting interviews. "No shit? Brookings was army infantry? How the hell did we miss that?"

I shake my head. "No. They were in basic training together, then after those eight weeks were up they went their separate ways. Brookings was actually a reservist, but they do basic with the regular army guys. After that, once Brookings put in his time as a weekend warrior, he was a civilian all the way."

"Do we know anything about their time together?" Nate asks. "Any disputes, fist-fights, arguments over a girl?"

"I don't know; I'm following up on that now with the general. But he said that unless there were some serious disciplinary measures taken, there probably wouldn't be a record of that specifically. We should also try and find other guys that were in that same unit. Maybe they'll remember some issues between Phelan and Brookings."

"Will do," he says. Then, "Phelan is definitely our boy."

I nod. "I know. But we still don't have anything solid. No DNA, no ballistics, no eyewitnesses, nothing."

"He ran off . . . consciousness of guilt."

"For all we know he's on a fishing trip. The fact that we don't know where he is won't get us anywhere with the prosecutor, never mind a jury."

"The victims include his army buddy and ex-wife. That's pretty compelling evidence, or some wild-ass coincidence."

"That's for sure."

"What else did you learn from the general?" Nate asks.

"That Phelan can hide out as long as he wants, especially if he's in the woods. Give him a couple of sticks and a toothbrush and he can live forever; he can make a three-course dinner using tree bark."

"We don't know he's in the woods," Nate says.

"We don't know anything."

"So let's stick with Brookings for the moment. Let's say he knew him, which seems logical at this point. Can't be a coincidence that they were in the same basic training unit. So what does that tell us?"

"That he must have had a grudge against Brookings, whether warranted or not," I say.

"So the same must be true for the other victims as well?"

"Probably, but not definitely. He could have liked the feeling of killing Brookings and decided to recapture the magic."

The phone rings and I pick it up. It's a member of our team, Sergeant Eddie Rosario, and his message is quick and to the point. "Lieutenant, we appear to have another victim. He's a gas-station owner in Sussex."

I get the specific information from Eddie and hang up. "Phelan is still recapturing the magic," I say to Nate. "We've got another one."

I inform Captain Bradley of the news and we head out to Sussex, a small town in Northern New Jersey. The drive would ordinarily take an hour, but we make it in forty-five. Not that there is any great reason to hurry; the perpetrator will be long gone, and his handiwork is not going anywhere. Besides, the place is no doubt already swarming with cops.

By the time we get there, state cops have

secured the scene and the forensics people are doing their jobs. The location of the shooter is being pinpointed, and witnesses, few though they may be, are being questioned.

The gas station is in the middle of a wide-open area, which would have given the shooter few potential hiding places. In this sense it is different than the other killings, all of which afforded the shooter the ability to remain unseen.

The other side to this, of course, is that this is a very rural area, which means that there would have been very few witnesses around. Still, if Phelan shot from an area within view, there is always the possibility that someone saw him, even if he or she was not aware of the significance in the moment.

I interview a woman named Betty McCain, who is said to be the only known witness to the shooting, though not the shooter. Her Audi is still at the pump, but she is sitting in the rear office of the station.

When we walk in, she is sobbing quietly. It's understandable, but not a good sign for a promising interview.

"Ms. McCain, are you all right? Would you like something to drink?"

"I saw it happen. Please, can I go home?"

"I'm very sorry. No one should have to go

through that. My name is Lieutenant Brock; I'm with the state police. What is important now is that we catch the person who did this. So we need your help right now; in these situations, time can be of the essence. I just have a few questions to ask you, and then I will have someone accompany you home."

She nods. "Richard was about to say something, and then there was blood everywhere."

"I understand," I say. "Let's start at the beginning. Can you tell me what happened from the moment you approached the station?"

She pauses for a short while, as if gathering herself, and then tells the story. She pulled into the station, waited a few seconds for the owner to come out to pump her gas, and then she watched his chest explode in blood.

"He had a look on his face," she says. "It wasn't like he was in pain, it was more confusion, as if he just thought it was strange, and he couldn't understand what was happening. I will never forget that look."

I ask her if she saw anything unusual before she got to the station, anything that seemed out of the ordinary. She says no, that it was just an ordinary day and an ordinary drive. "I still had half a tank, but I always get gas on Tuesdays."

Her "Tuesday is gas day" revelation notwithstanding, there is not much to get from her. It's not because she is shaken up; she didn't see the shooter, which means she saw nothing that is important to us. Her story is identical to the witness reports at the tennis court and the hotel; they see the result of the shooter's handiwork, but not the shooter.

I tell her to wait here and that I will have someone drive her home in her car, with another car following. When I leave the office, Nate is just about to enter it.

"There's someone we need to talk to," he says.

"I saw this SUV up on Cashen road. It was just sitting there. Seemed strange to me."

We're talking to Robert Howell, a local resident who owns and operates the combination hotel and restaurant in town. When he heard about the shooting, he thought that what he had seen might be valuable.

"Maybe I should have done more," he continues. "Richard was my friend. Richard was everybody's friend."

"What color was the SUV?"

"White. Maybe off-white."

"Did you get a license plate? Do you know the make and model?"

He shakes his head. "No license plate, sorry. It never entered my mind. But it was a Ford Escape, probably five years old. I used to drive one myself; that's why I knew."

That's the kind of car that Phelan has, the kind we've been showing photos of in the media. "Why did it seem strange to you?"

"Well, it's not a road that's used much," he says. "I was only on it because an employee of mine had called in that her car wouldn't start. So I went to pick her up. But you can drive on that road all day and not see another car."

"So you saw it sitting there," Nate says. "Why did it seem strange?"

"Just the fact that it was there. There's nothing surrounding it; the only reason to leave a car there would be if it were disabled. But the hood wasn't up or anything, and why not just call for help? And I didn't see the driver walking anywhere. I mean, it wasn't anything that was amazing, it just seemed a little strange, that's all."

"So you looked to see if there was a driver in the car?"

He nods. "Absolutely. I stopped, because I thought maybe they were having car trouble. I was going to offer to help. The car was locked. I looked inside, but there was no one inside, at least not that I could see."

"We'd like you to take us there, please."

"Sure."

Nate takes Howell in our car; we bring four other officers with us, as well as a forensics team. It's a five-minute drive, but it winds up and around a hill. Finally, Howell points. "It was up there, maybe

174

fifteen feet past that tree."

We stop and walk over to the spot he is talking about. There are some faint tire tracks there, but the road is dusty, and the tracks could have been left by any car that passed by.

Phelan left nothing physical behind; I didn't expect that he would. But looking south, we can see that what he did leave us is his vantage point. About three hundred yards away, down a sloping hill, is Richard Decker's gas station.

I call Nate over and point. "He could have gone down that incline toward those bushes," I say. "He'd have an easy shot at the gas station, and no one could see him from the road unless they made it a point to go out of their way to look. Howell would have had no reason to do so."

I ask Howell where the road leads to.

"Really nowhere," he says. "At the end you can get on what they call the Widows Road. They named it that because they say that back in the day men went into the forest and never came out."

"So there's dense forest up there?"

He nods. "For sure. I mean once in a while people go in there to go camping and that kind of thing, but not too many. The only way to get in is to hike."

"Are there trails cut out?"

"I don't think so, but I'm not a hiker, so I could be wrong."

We drop Howell back at the station, and then Nate and I head back home. "It fits in with what the general said. He can hide in there forever and live off the land. Plus he could have brought in a whole SUV load of supplies."

Nate nods. "We need to check out the terrain. Maybe we can have choppers do surveillance."

"The thing that puzzles me is the car. He used it to get here, and he used it to shoot the gas-station operator."

"So?" Nate asks.

"So where the hell is it? Howell said there are no roads into the woods; we'll check it out, but he's probably right. And there sure as shit aren't any parking lots. So where's the car?"

"Maybe he's not in the woods, but he wants us to think he is."

"He's playing with us," I say. "He's playing with us."

The note is waiting for me when I get home.

It's just a copy; this one was delivered to the office, and forensics has already had their hands on it. Once again they got nothing off it.

It was mailed from a mailbox about three miles from Richard Decker's gas station, just up the road toward the New York border.

The note is longer than usual; Phelan is becoming less cryptic and more informative. It says:

"He's pumped his last gallon. But I'm afraid one at a time isn't getting it done. Too many victims left on the wall . . . so much to do, so little time."

"He mailed it yesterday," Jessie says. "Once again that means he knew exactly what he was going to do and was positive he'd be able to do it."

I nod. "It also means that if he's hiding

out in the woods, he's not afraid to come out. He could have sent the note today, before or after he shot Decker. But coming out twice didn't bother him."

"If he's in there, then he has to have a way in and out by car. He'd have to be in deep enough to be able to avoid detection. So if he didn't have the car in there, how is he getting to it so easily?"

"I wish there was some way of establishing communication," I say. "He's talking to me through these notes, but he's not giving us a way to talk back."

"You could talk through the media."

I shake my head. "That could provoke him and get him to show off."

"What do you think he's getting out of this? Settling old scores? Or just the thrill of killing and getting away with it?"

"Could be both. Right now we only have a connection between Phelan and Brookings, so that could have been some kind of revenge thing. But we have nothing on the others, except for Phelan's ex-wife, at least not yet. Of course, if I could have made the Phelan-Brookings connection two years ago, there wouldn't be any others."

"How do you figure that?"

"Well, I'm just guessing here, because I can't remember a goddamn thing, but if I had uncovered the connection back then, I would have nailed Phelan with it. I would have gone after him much harder, instead of just letting him walk."

"He went to prison, Doug."

"That had nothing to do with me, and all it did was give him time to plan all this. We covered his room and board while he decided on his victims."

"Don't go there."

"Where?" I ask.

"To that place where you blame yourself for something that is not your fault."

"That's easy for you to say."

"No, it's not. But it is necessary. I have seen this movie; I know how it ends."

She doesn't have to spell it out more clearly. Last time I went to "that place," I withdrew from the world to the point where I broke off my engagement to Jessie. That doesn't feel possible this time, not to me, but I can certainly understand her viewing it differently.

Basically the only thing that gave me a fresh chance with her was getting shot and losing my memory. I'm going to try to avoid a repeat of that.

"I'm okay this time, Jessie. I can deal with it."

"You'd better, or this time I'll shoot you

myself."

"You're a delicate flower," I say.

"Thank you. Now get back to catching a mass murderer. That message was pretty clear."

"Certainly was. And I have no doubt he wouldn't hesitate to change his method of killing."

"Are you sending teams into the woods to look for him?"

I've thought about it, but it doesn't make sense right now, and I tell her so. "We don't even know that he's in there, and it's not like there's just one specific area. There are a whole bunch of forests up there. We wouldn't have nearly the manpower to cover it, and based on his training, our people could probably walk right past him and not know it."

"What about choppers?"

I nod. "We'll probably try it, but those woods are dense. My guess is nothing will come of it."

The phone rings and Jessie answers it. After listening for just a few seconds, she puts me on.

"Lieutenant, this is Sergeant Rankin. I'm manning the tip line, and we've got one you might want to hear. I could patch him through."

"Okay, do so. But stay on the line after you do."

In just a few seconds, I hear a click, and Rankin says, "Lieutenant, this is Mr. Scott Holman. Mr. Holman, tell the lieutenant what you told me."

"Well, I was watching the press conference on television, the one that said Helen Mizell was one of the victims and that Danny Phelan was a suspect."

"And?"

"Well, I didn't know if you knew, and I thought I'd call to make sure, but Mrs. Mizell was a teacher, way back in the day, at Englewood High."

This guy is taking a long time to get to the point. "And?"

"Well, I'm pretty sure Danny was in her class."

I call Nate and tell him the news about Helen Mizell.

"Damn," he says. "Between her and Brookings and his ex-wife, there must be these connections between Phelan and every victim. And some of them are weird. His high school teacher? Maybe she gave him a *C,* so he waits twenty-five years and kills her? When I had a teacher that gave me a *C,* my parents sent her flowers."

"Jessie is confirming that this Holman guy is correct."

"Should be easy enough for her to do," he says. "He kills his high school teacher, and a guy he was in basic with? We are dealing with a major whacko."

"As opposed to a normal, well-adjusted guy who hides in the trees and shoots people?" I ask.

As if on cue, Jessie calls and tells me that Holman, in fact, was right; Helen Mizell taught at Englewood High, and Phelan was there at the time. She hasn't yet confirmed that he actually had her as a teacher, but that doesn't matter. The simple fact of the connection has already exploded the co-incidence meter.

I had asked Nate to assign detectives to do a deep dive on the late Mrs. Mizell. We'll talk to any family we can find, including the two sons who apparently had little to do with their mother. Any friends, and especially former fellow teachers, will be on our radar as well. It is not likely to help us catch Phelan, but will help with motive.

I call Nate back. "Anything on Brookings?" I ask, since we've done the same deep dive on him.

"I was just checking. Our people talked to three other guys in the same basic-training unit. None of them remember any problems between Brookings and Phelan; two of them didn't remember Phelan at all."

I suggest that we start chopper runs over the woods north of Sussex; Nate agrees but thinks it unlikely that Phelan would be in an area where he'd be exposed to surveil-lance.

I feel the same way, but ask, "What's the downside? You got anything else to do with the choppers?" I know he understands this without my pointing it out, but I think I just like saying the word "choppers."

Nate goes off to get Bradley's authorization; even though Nate and I like to talk about choppers, we don't have any actual authority over them. Meanwhile, I'm heading to Scott Holman's house to talk about Helen Mizell.

Holman lives in Leonia, on a cul-de-sac, in a house with a manicured lawn. It defines suburbia and comfortable family living; my guess is that the Holmans have two-point-two children, one-point-one of whom has a dance recital and the other one-point-one plays Little League baseball.

I can see that in the back is a swing set and an aboveground pool, further confirming my assessment. I'm not judging it critically; for all I know there will come a point in the future that I might want the same thing. I don't know how far distant in the future that will be because I don't know how many decades it will take Jessie to trust me enough to marry me. And then by the time she would be willing to bear my child, her biological clock would have long ago stopped ticking.

I ring the bell and in less than a second I hear a dog's barking. It sounds like high-pitched yapping, and when the door opens

I understand why. Holman is standing there holding a little white fur-ball that can't be more than five pounds. Bobo could literally have this dog for lunch and get most of him stuck between his teeth.

Holman smiles. "Sorry, Bruiser doesn't like strangers," he says.

"That dog is named Bruiser?"

He nods. "We were going for incongruity."

"You achieved it."

He laughs and invites me in. He offers me something to drink, and when I ask for water, he goes off and comes back with the water and without Bruiser.

Once we're settled in, I say, "Thanks for calling in; we appreciate it."

"No problem. I was a little bit freaked out about it, and I figured maybe you didn't know."

"Can you remember anything about either Helen Mizell or Danny Phelan, especially any issues between them, that might be helpful to us?"

He shakes his head. "I've been wracking my brain, but I can't come up with anything. I think I had her for one class, and I don't even know if Danny was in it. It's been a while, longer than I want to admit."

"What recollections do you have of each

185

of them, separate from each other?"

"Well, Mrs. Mizell, she taught English Lit and was considered a tough grader, so no one wanted to get into her class. She also talked really low, very hard to hear, so we called her Hollerin' Helen."

I say, "There goes that incongruity thing again."

He laughs. "Right . . . I guess I haven't grown much over the years. Anyway, I didn't know her much at all, but I knew Danny reasonably well. I mean we weren't best friends or anything, but we had a lot of friends in common. And we were both on the baseball team. He was a good guy. Low key, funny, but pretty tough. I think most of the kids liked him, but they wouldn't have wanted to mess with him."

"Can you think of people he might have had disagreements with? Maybe got into fights with, verbal or physical?"

"Not really. Like I said, he was a good guy. I was really surprised when I heard about him going to jail for the drug stuff, and this latest thing, this just blew me away. I mean, I know you never really know about people. I've seen the neighbors on TV who say, 'Gee, I never imagined he would kill all those people with a hatchet; he seemed so nice and quiet.' But with Danny, it's really a surprise."

"Are there people you are in touch with, from back in high school, who might also have associated with Phelan?"

"Sure."

"We might like to talk to them. If you could make a list, with contact information if you have it."

"Boy, did you come to the right place."

"What do you mean?"

"We're having our twenty-fifth reunion Friday night at the Colonnade Restaurant in Park Ridge, they've got like a ballroom there. I'm one of the chairmen of the committee, so I have contact information for almost everyone in the class."

"Can you send me an electronic copy?"

"I'll send you everything I've got on the reunion, including all the contact info," he says, and I give him my email address. Then I thank him and get up to leave.

"I'm sure you deal with this all the time," he says. "But for a guy like me, with a family, it's scary. Makes me feel vulnerable."

"You'll be fine; you've got Bruiser."

Deirdre Clemons probably experienced three or four seconds of abject terror.

A librarian in a rural area about eight miles north of Sussex, she always left work promptly at 6:00 P.M., and this day was no exception. She could have left earlier; there were literally no patrons there at the closing hour, but her job called for her to stay there until six, so that's what she did.

Deirdre had been concerned about the less frequent usage of the library facilities; it had been a gradual decline over the last few years. She was afraid that the county might cancel the funding, which in her mind would have been a tragedy. The next nearest library of any size was almost twenty miles away.

Deirdre was near retirement age, so she wasn't particularly concerned about losing her job, though she loved what she did. In fact, once she retired she'd probably volunteer there. It's just that she considered a library an absolutely vital part of every community, even communities that didn't take sufficient advantage of it.

Deirdre had heard about the horrible murder of the gas station owner not that far away, but it didn't make her more cautious. Everyone who lived in the area was so friendly that there just was no feeling of danger, even after what happened. On some level, Deirdre just assumed that the poor murder victim must have been involved in something untoward.

But when she left the building and started walking toward her car, alone in the parking lot, she did look around, just to be sure. She saw no one.

Deirdre got in the car, reached to turn on the ignition, and felt the arm around her neck. Three seconds later that neck was broken, and two seconds after that, she was dead.

This morning I'm back at the house of Cynthia Morris, Phelan's ex-wife.

The house has been locked up and guarded by cops ever since she was gunned down while getting her mail, but today a search warrant is being executed for the contents.

Helen Mizell and Walter Brookings had connections to Danny Phelan, albeit obscure ones. I have to assume that there was some discord or friction between the victims and Phelan that we just don't know about yet. It is probable that Mizell and Brookings weren't even aware of it, or had no recollection.

It could have been some real or perceived slight that took on a large significance in Phelan's warped mind, yet meant nothing to Mizell and Brookings. Certainly it was nothing that they thought they were going to die for.

If his notes to me are to be believed, and so far he's been backing them up, then Phelan has almost a hundred additional victims on his hit list. They might be people who he's carried similar grudges against over the years, all of whom he now plans deadly retribution against.

So we have to dig into Phelan's life and learn what we can. Maybe we can find something that will protect one of his targets, or even help apprehend him. More likely not, but, like sending up the choppers, there's no downside to trying.

Of course, in the murder of Cynthia Morris, there is no need to search for some hidden grudge. She divorced him and refused to take him back, so a reason for his resentment of her is out in the open.

I don't have an important role here today; the officers executing the warrant know what they're doing. They also know that they are not here to make value judgments about potential evidentiary value; if something could be of the slightest, remotest significance, they are to catalogue it and take it back to the station.

I'm standing out front when I get a call from Captain Bradley. "The FBI is entering the case," he says. "You know the drill. It doesn't change what we're doing, but we'll need to cooperate."

I've expected this; in fact, I'm surprised it took so long. "Under what jurisdiction?"

"Not that they need any, but if we think he's hiding in the woods in North Jersey, then those woods extend into New York. They view it as unlikely he would be observing state borders, so there is a credible reason to think he's traveled across them."

"The more the merrier," I say.

"Your very large partner was slightly less welcoming when I told him."

I actually have no problem with this development; if it helps to get Phelan off the streets, I'm all for it. "I have a smaller ego than Nate," I say.

"You have a smaller everything than Nate. How's it going at the ex-wife's house?"

"A barrel of laughs. I'm coming back in. . . ." I stop because a car pulls up and Julie Phelan gets out. She's alone, and she looks angry as she walks toward me. I hope I can get my knees to stop shaking before she gets here.

"Lieutenant, what is going on here? This is my house now."

"Captain, let me call you back." I hang up and hand Julie the paperwork I have in my pocket. "And this is my search warrant. It is lawful and we are executing it. I'm afraid you're not welcome to be inside while we do it."

The aggression seems to seep out of her, but she still can't let it go. "What do you want from my mother? Can't you let her rest in peace?"

"We don't want anything from your mother. We want to know if there are any possessions of your father's in there, any paperwork, old photographs, etc."

"There aren't."

"You're sure of that?"

"Yes. Why do you want them?"

I'm torn here; my inclination is to get rid of her and not tell her anything. For all I know she might be in contact with her father, though our phone taps have not turned up anything. But I also can use her help.

So I decide to give it a shot.

"Come with me," I say. "Please."

"Where to?"

"To that bus stop bench over there. We need to talk."

She looks like she is going to resist, but then nods and follows me to the bench. I sit down, and she sits as far from me as possible without falling off the side. "My father is innocent," she says.

"There is a lot of evidence that says

otherwise. We have found a connection between some of the people who died and your father. I expect we'll find the same is true for the others."

"No."

"Yes, Julie. That's why I'm here. That's why we're going through this. We need to stop the killings."

"He wouldn't be doing this."

"If he's innocent, that will come out, I promise. But he ran away, so we have to assume the worst. At least until we learn otherwise."

She nods. "Okay. I understand that."

"His belongings, his papers . . . they weren't in his house. How is it you're so sure they aren't here?"

She's quiet for a little while, looking down at the ground. "Because I have them. Mom didn't want to have anything to do with him; she was going to throw everything out. So I took it. A friend of mine let me keep it in his garage; it's only a few boxes. Then when I moved out, I put it in storage; that's where it is now."

"Will you give it to me?"

"I can't."

"Julie, I'm going to share something with you. Back a couple of years ago, when the first shooting happened, I had reason to suspect your father. So I interviewed him, and I investigated him, and I decided he was not the killer."

"So why can't you have been right?" she asks.

"Maybe I was, maybe not. But if I was wrong, if he did it and I didn't make sure he was arrested for that crime, then all of the killings since are my fault. Do you understand? I very much do not want him to have done this, but I have to know. I can't let more people die."

She stares at the ground a while longer and finally nods. "Okay, but I'll give it all to you. No one else."

"Fair enough. Where is it?"

"I'll get it and turn it over to you."

"Thank you, Julie. You're doing the right thing."

"How come it doesn't feel like it?"

She tells me that it might take a day or so because she wants to go through the stuff before turning it over.

"Don't edit it," I say. "You never know what might be of value to the investigation."

"I won't. I just want to keep anything valuable, especially if it's of sentimental value. You get everything else."

I want to ask her if she called Phelan to tell him about her mother's death, an event which sent him on the run. It wouldn't mean anything if she did, since I assume he fired the fatal shot, so he would obviously have known all about it. But if she said that she didn't, it would be further proof of his guilt, since there is no other way he could have known.

I don't ask her that or any other questions right now. I've got what I wanted from this conversation. She trusts me, and I don't want to screw that up before I get the materials I want.

"The deceased, whose name is being withheld, was in the driver's seat," the local news announcer is saying as I turn on the television. He continues, "It is unclear, or at least the authorities aren't saying, what the exact cause of death was."

"Why do we watch the news in the morning?" Jessie asks. "It's always so depressing. Why don't we wake up to music?"

She's got a point. The announcer is talking about a woman found dead in her car near the northern New Jersey border with New York. The car somehow caught fire, though the cause of the fire is not known. At least according to the announcer, there was no apparent crash.

When the firemen arrived, the flames had mostly run their course, and of course it was too late to save the woman. I'm sure there are other excruciating details, but for the moment we are spared them. A reporter

197

is on the scene, and there are photographs of the burnt-out shell of a car.

"We're homicide detectives," I say. "We watch the news to find out what my day will be like."

"You're off the hook on this one," Jessie says. "I'll bet she was smoking in the car and fell asleep."

"Why didn't she wake up and open the door?"

"Maybe she was on drugs and had passed out."

"I think that's near Sussex," I point out.

"You think this could be our boy?"

"No, not unless he's completely changed his MO, which seems very unlikely. This was hands on; our boy likes to take out his victims from a safe distance."

That conversational area exhausted, Jessie asks if I'm going to take Bobo for a walk.

"Bobo takes me for a walk," I say. "He just goes where he wants to go; I don't think he even notices I'm holding the leash. As far as he's concerned, I'm only there to pick up his shit."

"Let's go together," she says. "Like a family. You going to shower first?"

"I refer you to my previous comment about picking up Bobo's shit. That doesn't really feel like it should be a post-shower operation."

So Jessie gets the leash, I get the bag, and off we go. We make the perfect family . . . a boy, a girl, and their very hairy horse.

I, of course, spend the entire walk thinking about our search for Danny Phelan. I'm anxious to get the materials that Julie is going to turn over to us, although I'm not naïve enough to think there will be a smoking gun, literal or otherwise, in there.

The material is by definition old; Phelan has been away and hasn't added to it in a long while. There's not going to be a diary that lists his future victims in order, but maybe there will be some reference to those he has already targeted, some hint of grudges that he might hold.

I know that Bradley and those above him are feeling tremendous pressure. It's not a game to them, but it is a fact of life that catching Phelan will be considered a "win." Every day with him on the run is a "loss," and the losses are mounting.

For me, and for Nate, it's a different kind of pressure. Phelan is not going to stop killing; he's made that all too clear. So every day that goes by with him on the loose is a day that we just might get a phone call saying that someone else is dead.

And every time we get one of those calls,

all I can think about is that the victim would be alive had I not let Phelan slip through my fingers last time.

We get back from our walk and feed Bobo. That in itself is quite a sight to behold; he eats like Nate, but without using his hands — or in his case, paws. Jessie makes sure not to overfeed him; she wants to control his weight because in a dog his size, there is a danger of hip issues. And Bobo would be very easy to overfeed; he would eat a filing cabinet if she offered it to him.

Just like Nate.

We head down to the station. On the way I get a report that the choppers, as expected, have not turned up anything in the woods. There have been a few false alarms that they've checked out, but they've either been animals or campers.

We've got our morning meeting with the team coming up, during which we give out assignments and discuss any potential or real developments. Nate and I take turns running the meeting, and fortunately, it's his turn today. I'm not big on public speaking, even when it's not really in public, when I've essentially got nothing to say.

But I stand up near the front with Nate, to answer questions that might come up. Near the end of the meeting the side door opens and I see Captain Bradley signaling me to come over.

When I do, he closes the door behind us, so that we're alone in the hall. "Did you hear about the woman who died in the burning car up north?" he asks.

I nod. "Just from news reports."

"Well, she was apparently dead before the car burned. Her neck was broken."

I don't say anything; he'll get to his point quickly enough.

"So you and Nate better get up there," he says.

"It's our case?"

Bradley nods. "It's our case. The car that she was in, the SUV that burned, is a Ford Escort belonging to one Danny Phelan."

The meeting is ending anyway, so I grab Nate and we head for still another murder scene.

A county cop, Detective Roy Chasman, knows we are coming and is waiting there for us. He's the one who got the VIN off the car and matched it to the APB we had out on Phelan.

The scene is still being guarded, but the event has long been over. The car had been consumed by flames; just the shell still stood there. Even so, it is obvious that it was an SUV.

The woman's body has also been taken away. If she was stuck in that inferno, there can't have been much of her left. The coroner's report said that the body was intact enough to tell that her neck was broken — not an injury that could be attributed to the fire. I hope his belief that she was dead before the fire started is accurate; the alternative is pretty awful.

"Her name was Deirdre Clemons," Detective Chasman says. "She was a librarian." Then, "I knew her; everybody around here knew her. She was as nice as they come." He shakes his head. "She was nice, and she was a librarian, and someone broke her neck and set her on fire."

"Is this where she was killed?" I ask.

"Hard to know. Best as we can tell, she left the library last evening, like always. But never got home."

"Did she have a car?"

"Yes, it's still in the library parking lot. So most likely she was grabbed there. Maybe killed there, maybe not."

"So he put her in this car," Nate said, "then came here, set it on fire, and left her."

Chasman nods. "And put gasoline all over the seats to make sure it burned. He was making a point of some kind."

"They were making a point," I say, with an emphasis on "they." "There had to be at least two of them. He could have driven to the library in the SUV, but once he set fire to it here, he would have needed a way to get back to wherever he's hiding out. He couldn't walk anywhere from here; this is too isolated. Someone had to have picked him up; otherwise he'd have been taking too great a risk. He didn't call Uber."

Chasman nods his agreement. "And because it's so isolated, we haven't found any witnesses. No one reported anything unusual so far, and we have cops canvassing the closest neighborhoods."

"Was she in the driver's seat?"

"Yes."

Nate says, "Nothing would have looked unusual until the moment he set the fire. He could have had her propped up in the seat, or lying down, until he lit it. And he wouldn't have made that move until he was sure there was no one around."

"Did she have a family?" I ask.

Chasman nods. "A husband, no children."

"Do you know him also? Because we're going to need as much detail on her background as we can get, to see if we can find a time when her path crossed with Phelan's. And when I say background, I mean starting in kindergarten and ending last night."

"I'm on it."

"Thanks. Can you take us to the library parking lot?"

We follow Chasman to the library, which is closed. I'm not sure if it's in honor of Ms. Clemons or whether it's to keep the area as pristine as possible. "No video surveillance here?" I ask, and he shakes his head.

The back parking lot cannot be seen from the street, there's a winding, uphill road that leads to it. "I bet his helper was here as well. That car was all over the news, and the gas station guy was killed not far away. If she saw the car, she might have been leery, or at least the killer might expect that."

"So where was the guy who grabbed her?"

"Hard to know," I say. "He could have been hiding near the door and either grabbed her there or held a gun on her. He even might have been in the back seat of her car."

Chasman nods. "Until now this was not an area where people had to lock their car a lot."

"Once he got her, then the SUV would have pulled up. But they had to have two cars here. The killer drove her in the SUV; she was probably dead by then. If you're going to kill her, might as well do it right away, in a place that's secluded. Then the helper followed in the other car."

"Cold-blooded bastards," Chasman says. He seems like a good, experienced cop, but I doubt he's seen many things like this. It takes a lot of getting used to.

On the way back, I say, "Something here

doesn't compute. We've got Phelan killing these people because of some weird grudges he's had. But if he's not doing this alone . . ."

"Right," Nate says. "What does the other guy get out of it? They both hate the same people? Or he's along for the ride? Doing Phelan a favor? Maybe we've been looking at this all wrong."

"But he killed his high school teacher; what else could he have gotten out of doing that?"

Nate has no answer for that, so we just drive the rest of the way in silence.

The note was delivered today, which is no surprise.

By the time I get home, Jessie has already had a forensics team out to the house. They opened it in her presence, and she copied down what it said for my benefit. Then they took the original back to the lab, where they will learn nothing from it.

The note says: "ANOTHER VICTIM GOES UP IN FLAMES. BUT SO MANY LEFT, AND SO LITTLE TIME. . . ."

I tell Jessie about the events of the day and then settle in to read the investigative reports that I wasn't around to see earlier. One of them has some significance. Alex Randowsky, the victim shot at the tennis courts, was a 50 percent owner of a restaurant in Englewood that Phelan was known to have frequented on occasion.

Randowsky was an investor and absentee owner; he had little to do with running the place. But so what? I have it all figured out: Phelan and his unknown accomplice ate there and didn't like the service. Maybe the soup was cold, or the waiter forgot to fill their water glass promptly.

So instead of not leaving a tip in protest, they murdered an investor in the restaurant.

Makes perfect sense.

I'm ready for bed at around eleven o'clock. Jessie is already in bed reading, which is a sure sign that it's up to me to give Bobo his nighttime walk. I would have done it anyway; with Phelan's preoccupation with me, I've followed Nate's advice and taken extra precautions.

One of those precautions, because I'm a chauvinist pig, is making sure that Jessie is not the one to walk Bobo at night. Phelan could be trying to get to me, and there would be no surer way to do that than go after Jessie.

I'm also walking a different route, going along the back alleys between houses in the maze that is our neighborhood. And I even go through different alleys each time, so as not to be predictable.

All of this keeps me from having to be on open streets that would provide Phelan with a clean shot, while at the same time giving Bobo new routes to explore and sniff. As an added benefit, it further assures Jessie that the reckless "old me" has matured into the careful, measured "new me."

Bobo has a rather strange idiosyncrasy: he likes to piss on garbage cans. He'd rather bust a bladder than piss on a fire hydrant or a telephone pole, but garbage cans set him off, and these alleys are full of them. I think he must drink a gallon of water in anticipation of our back-alley walks, because he doesn't miss a single one.

Unlike our walks on the street, these are at a very leisurely pace; it's a few steps and then a stop at a garbage can. So it's a mixed blessing. On the one hand, I don't get my arm pulled out of its socket. The downside is I spend a hell of a lot of time in alleys watching Bobo piss.

We're on the way back, going through different alleys than we took on our outbound route, when Bobo suddenly tenses, alert. I react, and I see the slight glint of metal about seventy-five feet away, around the side of a garage.

My instincts kick in and I dive behind a metal can — actually two cans side by side — pulling Bobo with me. As I'm doing so, I hear the shot, and the bullet hitting the back door of a house. I was standing in front of that door; I don't have the slightest doubt that had I not moved, that bullet would have exploded my heart.

Bobo saved my life.

For now.

As I pull out my revolver, another bullet comes crashing into the can. Fortunately it's sturdy, but I don't know how much more it can withstand. It moves back with the impact, and I steady it and keep it in place.

The noise is deafening against the silence of the night, as it rebounds off all of the structures in this relatively enclosed area. I peer out; I need to know where this guy is. Otherwise I have no chance of making it out of here.

The situation, when I get my bearings, turns out not to be as bad as I thought. While Bobo and I are pinned down and can't move without exposing ourselves to fire, Phelan is in a similar position. If he tries to get away without finishing the job, then I will see him and will have a clear shot. There's enough light from the houses to do the job.

Bobo does not want to be here, and it's all I can do to hold on to him. He's excited and anxious, panting and pulling on the leash. I think the gunshot sounds are freaking him out, and I can't say I blame him.

But if he ventures out where he could be seen at all, in the dim light Phelan might think it's me and take a shot at him. I need to protect him; the big dope saved my life. While keeping an eye on Phelan's position, I tie Bobo's leash to a hose bib that is on the house behind me.

I tie it as tight as I can, leaving Bobo very little room to move. It will piss him off, but I think it will hold — though I can't be sure. At Bobo's size, it would make more sense to tie him to a hitching rail in front of a Western saloon. But one way or the other, this is not going to take long. "Hang in, buddy," I whisper. "I'll get us out of this; you'll be pissing on garbage cans for many years to come." I'm talking to him and petting him to calm him down; I don't want him to use his strength to pull loose.

"You can't move, Phelan," I yell. "I can't either, but time is on my side; I've got all night. Give it up."

A voice responds, but it's not Phelan. "What's going on down there?" A guy in one of the houses has just opened a window and is calling down.

He is my solution.

"Call the police," I yell. "Report an officer-involved shooting that is ongoing. Then keep away from that window!"

He doesn't answer, but leaves the window immediately. I have no doubt he'll call the cops, and the balance of power will totally turn against Phelan when they get here. He's got to make a move before they arrive. I don't.

"The cavalry is on the way, Phelan!" I yell. "Give it up."

"Okay." He stands up, holding a rifle with an extended arm. "I'm done."

"Drop the rifle."

He does so, and the noise clangs and reverberates in the alleys. Once I see him do so, I stand up, my gun pointing at him. He walks a few steps toward me, still mostly shrouded in darkness, and I say, "That's far enough."

He stops, and I say, "Walk over there to that house, put your hands against the wall, and spread them."

But as he turns to do so, I see him make a sudden move. There's a gun in his hand, or at least a piece of metal that reflects light.

I fire, twice, and he's blown backwards and goes down.

I can hear the sirens in the distance as I walk toward Phelan. He's lying on his back. One of my bullets hit him in the heart, which one could say is his final irony.

There's no doubt that he's dead; but I

move closer to check his pulse anyway. I hear the noise of the cops approaching, but I'm not paying attention.

There is no pulse; he's dead.

He's also not Danny Phelan.

He's William Gero, the owner of the rifle range, and at least one M4.

Fortunately, among the first group of cops to arrive is Sergeant Juan Santana.

He's Englewood PD, which makes sense, since I just killed William Gero in an Englewood alley. I know Juan; I worked with him on a couple of operations maybe two years ago. He's a good guy with a terrific sense of humor.

The reason it's fortunate that he's here is that this way I don't have to lie on the ground, spread-eagled, while they figure out who the good guys and bad guys are. When cops show up and someone is standing in an alley with a gun, having just shot someone, they have a tendency to assume the worst until they find out otherwise. In this case, Juan knows otherwise.

One of the good guys, who is suddenly standing next to me, is Bobo. I had momentarily forgotten about him and not untied him, which is why I'm somewhat surprised to see him standing here. And also why I will owe someone money for a broken hose bib, which is rattling on the other end of his leash. I'm not surprised he pulled off the hose bib, but I'm a little surprised he didn't pull the house down with it.

I ask Juan to call Nate and Jessie, not necessarily in that order. Englewood PD is processing the scene, and there will be no reason for state cops to intervene. Not only is this local and something they are totally capable of handling, but since I'm a state cop, our taking over might give the appearance of impropriety.

I won't have any trouble convincing anyone what happened here, especially since there is an M4 rifle on the ground, about seven feet from Gero's body. There's also a revolver, which looks like a .38, about a foot from the body.

My hope is that the rifle will be tested and found to be the weapon used in the recent killings, going back to Brookings. I also hope that the .38 proves to be the weapon that killed Helen Mizell. They are not just my hopes; they are my expectations.

In any event, with all this weaponry on the ground, it will be obvious to any investigating body that Gero was not in the alley to take out the garbage.

Jessie arrives before Nate, since our house is so close. She hugs me and Bobo; my hug comes first, but I think his is a little bigger. Not that I'm keeping track.

I tell Jessie everything that happened, ending it with, "Bobo saved my life. That big, dumb dope literally saved my life. He will hold this over me forever."

This prompts Jessie to bend down and give Bobo another, even bigger, hug. Of course, bending is not really necessary, since he's as tall as she is. She throws in a couple of "you're the best boy" to him. Then she asks me, "Why is there a faucet tied to his leash?"

"Why are you asking me? Ask him."

Nate shows up along with Captain Bradley and about a dozen other state cops. I really appreciate the support, especially since once I give a statement, Bradley arranges for me to be able to go home, pending further questioning when the Englewood cops need me. Without his intervention, I could have been stuck there all night.

So Jessie, Nate, Bradley, Bobo, and I head back to our house. Jessie makes coffee for everyone except Bobo, who gets a two-biscuit reward for his efforts. Then, having received enough hero worship for the night, he goes off to sleep, and the rest of us talk about the significance of tonight's events.

Bradley says, "I understand a lot of this depends on the ballistics, but for the moment, let's assume they check out. The chance that they happen to be a different M4 and .38 is well off the possible-coincidence meter. So, assuming they are the guns we've been looking for, where are we?"

I answer first. "Well, it's fair to say that our shooter is dead. But it still leaves Phelan out there."

"Maybe he's out there because he was afraid he'd be arrested and convicted, even though he's innocent. Maybe he thought the odds were stacked against him, so he ran."

Jessie shakes her head. "There's too much to tie Phelan to this. Do we think that Gero coincidentally murdered Phelan's English teacher and a guy from Phelan's basic-training unit?"

"Let's not forget Phelan's ex-wife," I point out.

"Actually, there's one more thing," Bradley says. "We just got the report about a half hour before I came here. The gas station owner that was killed, Richard Decker . . . he was in a car accident about six years ago. He pulled out in a parking lot without looking and hit Phelan's car."

Jessie frowns. "And that turned out to be worthy of a death sentence."

"We figured that there were two of them," Nate says. "One person couldn't have pulled off the murder of that woman from the library. So we know that Phelan is still out there, and his buddy is the latest victim of Wyatt Earp over here." He points to me, so as not to leave any doubt that I am the Wyatt Earp he is talking about.

I turn to Nate. "You're the next notch on my gun, you fat piece of shit."

Nate feigns a wounded look. "Captain, can't you suspend him for that? He demeaned a fellow officer."

"You're both idiots," Jessie points out, and nobody argues with that.

"There are two things I don't understand," I say. "Actually, there's a lot more than two, but I'm talking about the two main ones. The first is: What did Gero have to gain from this? Phelan's got the ridiculous grudges, but why Gero? Mrs. Mizell can't have flunked both of them in English 101."

"We'll dig into his history tomorrow, but maybe he just gets off on shooting people," Nate says.

I shake my head. "I don't think so. If that

was it, he wouldn't have been out of commission while Phelan was in jail. He didn't need Phelan to find victims, and he didn't need them to be people Phelan didn't like. He could have picked people out at random. But he waited for Phelan to be released before he started shooting again."

"I don't see how it could have been for money, either," Bradley says. "Phelan does not appear to have any."

I nod. "But Gero definitely did Phelan's dirty work, so he must have had a reason. And now we'll get to see if Phelan will pick up the slack."

"What's the other thing you don't understand?" Jessie asks.

"Why they went after me at all, but especially why now? I was their foil; they were having fun playing with me, mocking me. Why take me out? It's not like I was close to nailing Phelan. I wish that was the case, but we know it's not."

"You're a name," Nate says. "You're a media star. They hit you, and the media attention gets even bigger than it is now. They're stepping up their game."

Bradley nods. "I'm going to have a black-and-white on your street twenty-four/seven. If they came at you once, they can do it again. I think Nate is right."

"I think we should get engaged."

We're up, showered, dressed, and about to leave for the station when Jessie drops this bomb. As sentences go, this one is about as expected as her saying that she was just named starting right tackle for the Green Bay Packers.

"You do?" I ask.

"Yes. Why do you look so surprised?"

"Because every time I suggest getting married, you break into a cold sweat and start shaking violently. Then, when you've had a few minutes to think about it, you say, 'No . . . absolutely no . . . no chance.' I'm paraphrasing here."

"Who said anything about getting married?" she asks. "I said we should get engaged."

"I thought one followed the other."

"It didn't last time."

I'm not sure Jessie will ever get over the

fact that I broke up with her after being engaged. It was before I was shot and lost my memory, and before I re-fell in love with her.

"I know that, but this is the new me. The old me was an idiot."

"No argument there," she says. "Anyway, I think we should get engaged."

"I totally agree, but I'm just curious why you've come to this conclusion now."

"I've been thinking about that myself," she says. "I'm really not sure, but it might have something to do with you getting shot at in the alley. You obviously could have been killed, and it's not the first time and won't be the last. You have a dangerous job."

"And getting engaged will make me safer?"

"No, but it would get me into the obituary as the grieving widow."

I shake my head, sensing an opening. "Being engaged doesn't make you a widow."

"True, but I could at least be the grieving fiancée. Grieving ex-girlfriends don't make the obituary at all. I deserve better than getting shut out like that."

"This is a beautiful moment," I say. "Uplifting, really."

"So are you going to propose?"

"When? Now?"

"I could change my mind. But it's your call; I can't make decisions for you."

"Since when?"

"You going to do it or not?" she asks.

"Okay, but I didn't get you a ring yet."

"I'll accept an IOU on that."

I get down on one knee. Bobo thinks something is going on and wants to be a part of it, so he comes up next to me and sits on his backside, front legs up. Jessie starts laughing at the sight of me next to this enormous black hairball, who towers over me in this position.

"It's not funny," I say. "This is a very serious, vulnerable moment for me."

She wipes the smile off her face. "Okay. Sorry. Do your speech; convince me."

"Jessie, I love you and want you in my life forever. I also want you in my obituary. Will you engage me?"

She doesn't answer right away, seeming to ponder how to reply. Then she says, "I don't know what to say . . . this is so sudden."

I nod. "I know, but I'm a spontaneous person. The idea just came to me in the moment."

My knee is hurting, so I start to stand up, but she says, "Stay." Bobo and I both obey the command. Then she ponders some more, and then, finally, "Yes, I will engage you."

"Can I rise and kiss the potential bride?"

"You may."

So I get up, as does Bobo, but I'm the only one who gets to kiss Jessie.

"Not bad," she says. "Let's go to work."

The work part of the day does not appear to be starting well.

Jessie and I, newly engaged as we are, arrive at the station at seven thirty and already waiting for me is James McKinney, Julie Phelan's fiancé. I have no idea if she agreed to get engaged to him so she could get in his obituary, but this may not be the best time to ask him.

He's got a look on his face that is somewhere between very anxious and distraught. I think he looks worse than me, and I spent the night getting shot at.

I start with "Good morning," but it doesn't seem to take. "There's no chance of that," he says. "Julie is missing."

"Missing how?"

"She never came home last night."

I nod and invite him back to my office. Nate won't be in yet; he usually comes in at eight. But there's no need to wait for him; I can fill him in later.

I grab a cup of coffee on the way, but Mc-Kinney doesn't want any. When we get to the office and are settled, I say. "So Julie did not come home last night. Has this happened before?"

"Never. Not once."

"Do you have any idea where she might be?"

He hesitates, then, "I think she might be with her father."

That's what I was afraid of. Julie must have had second thoughts about cooperating with us and instead chose her father. I'm not happy about it, that's for sure, but I'm not surprised.

"Why don't you start at the beginning?"

He nods. "Okay, just forgive me if I ramble a bit; I'm pretty upset. Julie talked to me yesterday; she said she was going to give you some of her father's things. Notes or something."

I just nod, more as an encouragement to keep him talking than a confirmation of what he is saying.

"I said that was a good thing, that it would be best for everyone if she did that. I said whether he was guilty or innocent, the running needed to stop, that it couldn't end well."

He pauses, then, "Well, that set her off. All I was doing was agreeing with her approach, and suddenly I was the enemy. She screamed that I wasn't being supportive of her or her father, that everyone was against them.

"Then I got upset. I told her that she was damn right I wasn't being supportive of her father, that I thought he was a murderer. And that I was going to go to the police and tell them what I know. Then she screamed at me and left."

"And you haven't heard from her since?"

"No. I kept calling her, but she didn't answer her cell. Then I went to the office for a little while; there was a meeting I needed to be at. When I got home, I saw that her suitcase was gone. I think she must have come home and taken some of her things. Not nearly all, but some."

"You've tried calling this morning?"

A nod. "Of course. Every ten minutes. Twice while I was standing outside here, waiting for you. Her phone is turned off. I've called her friends; I've checked some of the local hotels . . . nothing. I think she might be with her father."

My worry here, which I don't share with him, is not that she left him. The health of their relationship is not on my list of concerns. I don't care if he lost Julie, but I'm afraid that I have. She was going to be my key connection to Phelan, past and present.

"You said you told her that you would go to the police and tell them what you know. What were you talking about?"

A pause, as if he's deciding how to answer. This could be getting interesting. "I think I know where her father is. Maybe where she is now."

The door opens and Nate comes in, holding a cup of coffee. "Sorry, didn't know you had company," he says when he sees me with McKinney.

"Can you give us a minute, Nate?" I don't want this conversation interrupted, and I have no doubt Nate will pick up on that.

"Sure. I'll be in Kinsler's office if you need me." He closes the door behind him as he leaves.

"You were saying that you might know where she is."

He nods. "I have a cabin; it's up near Great Gorge. It's been in the family for years, but I hardly ever go there. Technically it's owned by my brother, but he lives in San Francisco so he never uses it. It's very secluded, basically in the middle of nowhere."

"Julie has been there?"

He nods. "Yes. Once."

"What about her father?"

"I don't know if he's ever been there before; I don't think so." Another pause, then, "But I think he might be there now."

"Why do you say that?"

"First I want to know if Julie could get any trouble for this. I mean, if she's with him."

"I can't answer that. I would think they'd make allowances for her situation."

He nods in vigorous agreement. "Right. I mean, she's his daughter. She loves her father, no matter what he might have done. She thinks he's innocent."

"James, no matter what the situation, it will only get worse with time. You told her that yesterday, and you were right. This has to end now."

"You're right."

"So why do you think her father might be in your cabin?"

"Because Julie told him about it."

"When?" I ask.

"Last week. You weren't after him then. I thought it might be a good place for him to get away, not run away. He was under a lot of pressure, and I thought it might help him. So I mentioned the possibility to Julie."

"What did she say?"

"That he was innocent, and that he would never have to run away. But once he did, there's a chance he took her up on the idea. I don't know that, of course, but I wouldn't be surprised."

"We'll need you to tell us where it is, and describe the setup for us."

"I will." Then, "Julie will never talk to me again."

I don't respond to that, for two reasons:

He's probably right, and, either way, I don't really give a shit.

This time the note comes to Nate.

It says: "Too bad about your partner. He doesn't count toward the total . . . I threw him in as a bonus. Watch your fat ass, Nate."

Nate and I are reading the copy of it that forensics just delivered back to us. "He was pretty confident he'd get you," Nate says.

"He didn't count on the Bobo factor."

"This could change his MO. Gero was the marksman; we don't know that for sure about Phelan."

"Unless there's a third player," I say. "They could have a deep bench. But he's shown flexibility anyway. Deirdre Clemons got her neck broken before the car fire. That was up close and personal."

"He could come after you again," Nate says. "What happened last night might just piss him off."

"The captain already has security around our house, even though I think it's not necessary. But in any event, the note says you're the target now," I point out. "And he's obviously familiar with you; he knows you have a fat ass."

Right now James McKinney is off in another office with our tactical team. They are debriefing him on everything about the cabin . . . location, terrain, access roads, etc. Then I have no doubt that they will do aerial surveillance, probably with drones, to confirm everything. McKinney says that he has not been there in a long time, so we'll want to make sure that all his information is up-to-date.

We want to move fast on this, but we want to make sure we do it right. The great UCLA basketball coach John Wooden said, "Be quick, but don't hurry." That's the goal here.

Meanwhile Jessie and her team are gathering as much information as they can on William Gero. They had done some work on this previously, but stopped when Nate and I interviewed him and basically eliminated him as a suspect.

I seem to have a tendency to clear suspects who then go on to kill people; that's probably not a great trait for a homicide detective. I did it with Phelan a couple of years ago, and then repeated the maneuver recently with Gero. Maybe I'm in the wrong line of work.

I know that we've already served a warrant on Gero's rifle range for its records. We'll want to see if Phelan has ever been a customer of the place; his connection to Gero could be as simple as that. They could have met there and found they shared a love of guns and killing people.

Bradley is giving a televised press conference this morning; he's started to publicly refer to them as "updates." He hates doing them, but early on he promised transparency to the public, and the problem with that is it then requires him to be transparent.

Nate and I are sitting this one out; there is just too much going on here. But Bradley is joined by the police commissioner, who wants to share in the glory that one of the bad guys has been killed. Of course, the news is not all good . . .

"I know there has been media speculation," Bradley says as we watch on TV, "that the man who was killed in an attack on one of our officers is connected to the case. I am here to confirm the accuracy of that report. The deceased's name was William Gero, and pending ballistic and other tests, we believe that he has been involved in the recent spate of killings.

"I do want to point out, however, that Daniel Phelan remains a person of interest in the case. We believe that Mr. Phelan and others at the very least have information that is important to us. So I would like to implore everyone to remain vigilant, and to report anything that seems to be connected to our tip line.

"I wish I could stand here and say otherwise, but we do not consider this investigation to be concluded. Danger remains, and everyone should behave accordingly."

While Bradley is talking, the report comes in that the rifle and handgun that Gero had last night are, in fact, the weapons that were used in the killings. Of course, there is no absolute guarantee that Gero was the person pulling the trigger in those cases, but it seems like a pretty safe bet.

For now all we can do is wait for the tactical team to finish debriefing McKinney and then come to us with their plans. As the officers in charge, we will have the ability to revise those plans before implementation, but if we do, it will likely just be adjustments around the edges. This is what these people do for a living, and they simply are better at it than we are.

They finally finish with McKinney and

send him back out to us to see if we have any more questions for him. I ask him if he knows where Julie stored her father's material, since she is not around to turn it over as promised.

He says that he does not, though I don't know if he is telling the truth. He keeps expressing concern about Julie's reaction to his coming to us, saying, "I hope she understands that I'm just doing what's best for her."

My view of this, though it is not one formed from experience, is that a woman is likely to take a dim view of her boyfriend turning her and her father in to the police. It would seem that they have not invented the couple's therapy that could successfully deal with that situation.

The truth is that I still don't much care either way. I just want to find Julie Phelan — mostly because it will likely lead us to her father, but also because she might be in danger herself. Phelan may well be unstable; he's certainly nuts.

I send McKinney off with the admonition to try and find out what storage facility Julie Phelan might have used for her father's stuff. He says that he will, but I don't believe it.

I think he's going to wait and see what

comes out of our getting to his cabin, and then go from there.

That's exactly what I'm going to do as well.

There is only one road leading to McKinney's cabin.

Actually, calling it a road might be giving it too much credit. It is unpaved, narrow, and being encroached on by the shrubbery along the sides. It is probably better defined as a hiking trail wide enough for a car. Phelan's SUV, at least before it went up in flames, could probably have gotten through, but not without incurring some scratches.

So setting up roadblocks in a conventional sense is not exactly challenging. More difficult is making sure that if our targets get away, they don't escape into the dense woods.

The location of the cabin is a bit of a surprise to me, since it is quite a ways from the scenes of the murders at the gas station and library. I would have thought that Phelan would have slipped in and out to commit the crimes, but that is not the case.

Of course, at least in the case of the gas station, he may not have been there at all. Chances are William Gero pulled the trigger, and the job would not have required a second-in-command. The murder of the librarian is a different story; that was a two-person job.

So while we will have officers stationed at various points at the edge of the woods, they are not likely to see any action. If Phelan gets away, he is likely to go farther into the woods, where he will count on his survival skills to . . . well . . . survive.

That might be more challenging if Julie is with him, and if he cares about her. Moving with her in the woods, and hiding with her, would be considerably more difficult. Possible, but not ideal for him.

Working in our favor is that there is a considerable clearing outside the cabin on all sides. A lot of trees died in the making of that place. We will have aerial support when we go in, and they will have a clean shot at Phelan if he makes a break for it.

The heat-detecting machine is not an option here; we wouldn't be close enough to use it before making our move. It also doesn't really matter; we are going to assume that Phelan and maybe Julie are in there and behave accordingly. If they're not, then no harm, no foul, and it wouldn't be the first time we've come up empty.

Nate and I are nominally in charge of the operation — emphasis on "nominally." The

SWAT team commander, Lieutenant Morrow, will run the show. I've worked with him, and he is as good as they get.

He and his team know the goal: Our first choice is to capture Phelan alive, our second choice is to take him out in a body bag. Julie is to be treated as complicit in Phelan's crimes until we know otherwise. If there is any threat to the life or well-being of the law-enforcement officers, lethal force is 100 percent authorized.

We move into position along with the SWAT team; in this case that position is on the road about three hundred yards from the cabin. A light rain is falling, but no one seems to notice or care. It would take a lot more rain to make the dirt road difficult to navigate, but even that wouldn't matter, because we're going in on foot.

Morrow comes over to Nate and me and asks, "Ready?" It's a rhetorical question and a sign of respect; he knows that we are ready when he says we're ready.

And suddenly we're ready. The team members start running at a brisk clip along the road toward the cabin. Nate and I fall in behind them, and as we do, I can hear the faint roar of the approaching choppers. It will be their role to prevent Phelan from escaping out the back and into the woods.

As we get closer the noise from the choppers is deafening. That's at least partially by design; it would frighten anyone on the receiving end of this invasion.

Up ahead I can barely hear yelling over the noise, but I don't hear any gunfire. I'm hoping that means that Phelan gave up rather than that there is no one in the cabin worth shooting.

Morrow and I are carrying two-way radios, and the plan is for Nate and me to wait at the edge of the clearing for the okay to come in. That signal does not come. Instead, Morrow opens the door to the cabin from the inside and gestures for us to come in.

Nate and I head in; if there is any danger, it has long since passed. When we reach the door, Morrow turns and walks back in, and we follow.

It is then that we see the body. It's a woman, but it's not Julie Phelan.

Pinned to her chest is a note. It says: "You should understand by now that I am everywhere and nowhere. I know everything and no one is safe. You can tell that to Mr. McKinney."

The dead woman has been identified as Ruth Dempsey.

She is a resident of Carlyle, a town less than three miles from the cabin where she was found. The cause of death was strangulation; there was no skin under her fingernails and no evidence she was able to put up a fight. It is most likely that she was grabbed from behind and never had a chance.

My guess is that Phelan picked Ms. Dempsey at random; she was a handy victim because of her proximity. Her life was of no consequence to Phelan; he was simply using her to make a point.

The time of death, as estimated by the coroner, is very interesting. Ms. Dempsey is estimated to have been dead for eighteen hours before we found her. If that's accurate, then she was killed before McKinney even told us about the cabin.

Unfortunately, that decisively implicates Julie Phelan. McKinney told her he was going to go to the police and tell them what he knew. Julie and her father would then have known that the cabin was no longer safe, since we were about to find out about it from McKinney.

The only way that Phelan would have written that note vowing revenge against McKinney is if he learned the situation from Julie. Julie is therefore not a captive of her father, nor is she in danger from him. Whether or not she had anything to do with the previous killings — and I doubt that she did — her entire situation has changed.

Unless her father somehow forced her to reveal McKinney's plan to betray him, Julie is now part of this.

I call Bradley and tell him to put Julie's name and likeness out to the media, and he agrees to do so. No matter where they are, Julie is going to be a burden to Phelan as he both stays in hiding and ventures out to continue his killing spree. Maybe that will work in our favor.

Until the moment that we walked into the cabin, I was holding out the ridiculous hope, against all odds, that Phelan wasn't the killer. It was selfish of me because of my guilt for letting him go at the time of the

Brookings killing, but that's how I felt.

That hope is now effectively out the window.

I call James McKinney, who has not fared well in all of this. When he hears my voice, he quickly asks, "Have you found Julie?"

"Not officially," I say. "But she is on the run with her father. They had left the cabin before we got there."

"Shit," he says, not realizing that the bad news is still to come.

"There was another murder; a body was in the cabin."

"Who was it?"

"That's not important," I say. "Her identity will be announced at the proper time. But there was a message from Phelan; it was threatening toward you."

"Oh, no . . . oh, shit. Because I told you about the cabin?"

"I suppose so."

"Oh, man . . . how could he have known that?"

"I can't answer that. We can provide you protection. I can put an officer in front of your house twenty-four/seven."

He pauses for a moment before answering. Then, "I can't be holed up in my house all day. Dammit, I'm not the one who is supposed to be a prisoner."

"I'm sorry, it is what it is. Our goal is to get this behind us soon."

"I need to think this out," he says. "What about if I leave town?"

"What about it?"

"Do you think I'll be safe? Damn, I don't deserve this."

I feel badly for him; he did the right thing, and now he's scared to death. Which I guess is better than the other kind of death. "We can protect you," I say. "We can have you watched."

"You want me to be a target so you can trap Phelan," he says, not inaccurately. "That ain't happening, I can tell you that."

Nate walks in while I'm nearing the end of the phone call with McKinney and hears my end of it. "I assume he's not happy?" Nate asks after I hang up.

"You are a keen observer of the human condition. He's scared shitless."

He nods. "Can't say I blame him. Not only did he betray a mass murderer, but he also turned in the guy's daughter."

Time to change the subject. "Here's one of the many things that are worrying me: All along we've wondered how Phelan could be in hiding yet be mobile enough to be driving around and killing all these people."

"Now we know," Nate says. "He had Gero

to help do his dirty work. And now Gero is gone."

"Right. But what if it's not just Gero? If Phelan could have one accomplice, why not two?"

"No reason why not," Nate says. "But we can't even figure out what Gero had to gain from this. Isolated killing doesn't pay that well."

I nod. "The only way we are going to come close to finding out any of this is by learning how Phelan was connected to Gero in the first place."

Nate looks toward the door, so I do as well, and Jessie is standing there. "I think I've got your answer," she says.

"Gero and Phelan were in the army together," Jessie says.

"How do you know?" I ask, and I instantly regret the question when she gives me "the stare."

"Don't question genius," Nate says, then to Jessie, "Forgive him; he's young and stupid. Tell us more."

"I don't know much more. All I can tell you is that they were in the same place in Iraq at the same time. I can't put them together or give you any more details; that would be part of their army records."

I don't say anything; I just pick up the phone and call General Thielen. He's not available at the moment; I guess generals don't sit by the phone waiting for state cops to call. But I tell his assistant, Lieutenant Paul Anderson, that it is urgent that he call me back.

I don't say it's a matter of life and death

because that seems a little overdramatic, and besides, he knows I'm working on a murder investigation. "Life and death" sort of comes with the territory.

"Perhaps I can help you," Anderson says. "What is it you need?"

"Information."

"It would help if you could be more specific." When I hesitate, Anderson adds, "I can assure you that if General Thielen needs information to turn over to you, he will direct me to find it. So if you tell me now, I can get a head start on it, pending his willingness to provide it."

That makes a lot of sense to me, so I tell him what we need. I want confirmation that Gero and Phelan were actually in the same unit, and if so, firsthand information about their service and their relationship.

Lieutenant Anderson doesn't sound as if this is too daunting an assignment, and I assume that generals have their pick of who they want to work for them. So I've got some confidence that Anderson is a savvy guy, and he'll deliver. I hope it's fast.

While we're waiting, I ask Jessie if she has anything else to update us on. She will give us written reports, but if she has anything important, like the Gero news she's just delivered, she'll verbally tell us about it first.

"Not much," she says. "You'll be getting the reports. Most of it is background information on Helen Mizell."

"Did she rob banks while the kids were in homeroom?"

She smiles. "Nothing that exciting; in fact, nothing at all. Her husband died eleven years ago; he was an accountant. They had two sons, both semi-estranged from their mother. They live in St. Louis; I talked to one of them. He didn't have much to say.

"She left life insurance policies to three people; not huge, two of them were about two hundred thousand each. Those were for the sons, who even though they pretty much hated their mother, took the money. That's why I say semi-estranged."

"An obvious gesture of goodwill," I say.

She nods. "Touching. The third person, who she left less to, about fifty thousand, was a woman named Marcia Carnow. Not sure of the relationship; probably a cousin, but I'll know when we reach her, if we do. She also took the money."

"Any reason to think Mizell slighted Phelan in any way? Or even Gero?"

"None that I can find. And no way Gero was in her class; he went to high school in Greenville, North Carolina. That's where he grew up."

Nate suggests we go down to the cafeteria to get a cup of coffee. He's wanted to go down there a lot since they've been bringing in glazed donuts. We go along; we can talk as easily down there as here.

We no sooner get seated than the desk sergeant sends a guy down to tell me that there is a Lieutenant Anderson on the phone, waiting to talk to me. We go back upstairs, Jessie and I carrying our coffees, and Nate toting coffee and a bag of donuts.

"General Thielen has authorized my giving you the following information," Anderson says, seeming to choose his words carefully. "Gero and Phelan were in a specialized infantry unit together in Iraq in 2005."

"Good," I say. "What else have you got?"

"Nothing. The record doesn't speak to their relationship at all. But I can put you in touch with someone who should be more helpful. Major Lewis Taggart; he commanded the unit."

"Where is he?"

"Germany."

"That's not terribly convenient. Can you tell me how to get in touch with him?"

"I can patch you through. He's waiting for your call."

"Now?"

"Awaiting your assent."

"Lieutenant Anderson, you do nice work. Very impressive."

"Lieutenant Brock, when I speak for a general, it has a tendency to amplify my voice. Hold on for Major Taggart."

"Thanks for talking with me, Major Taggart."

"General Thielen," he says.

At first I think that he is saying that he is General Thielen, but I think he means that General Thielen's request is the reason he's talking. I suspect that this guy might speak a bit cryptically.

"Right. The general has been very helpful."

"It's eleven p.m. and I'm dining at the American embassy. Can we get on with this?"

"Of course. I'm looking for information about Daniel Phelan and William Gero. I understand you commanded their unit in Iraq."

"Information is an expansive word."

"Yes, it is." I realize that since he is in Germany, Taggart might not realize what has gone on here. It's all consuming for me, but not necessarily international news. I continue, "Phelan is a suspect in a number of murders, and Gero was an accomplice. Gero is now deceased; Phelan is at large."

"I'm aware," Taggart says, blowing my realization out of the water. "What kind of information do you require?"

"Do you remember them?"

"Yes."

"Were they both in the unit at the same time?

"Yes."

This is like pulling teeth; Taggart is acting like I'm charging him by the word. I decide to go more open ended with the questions; he's answering as if I'm cross-examining him.

"Major, we need to know about their service and specifically their relationship. You know what we're up against, so literally anything you can tell us about them in those days would be helpful."

"Fair enough," he says. "They were quite a group; all excellent, well-trained soldiers who unfortunately did not belong in the army. They were not prepared to accept discipline to the degree required in a combat zone, or in any zone in the military."

"What did they do that reflected their lack of discipline?"

"I suspected drug usage, which in and of itself would not have been wildly outside the norm. What got them in trouble, and ultimately led to Phelan being processed out of the military, was the after-hours difficulty that seemed to find them. Constant assaults, bar fights, that kind of thing."

"Can you describe the circumstances leading to Phelan being discharged?"

"Not really. He had left the unit by then."

That surprises me. "Why did he leave the unit?"

"What often happens is that soldiers within a unit like ours have specialties: medical, artillery, munitions, and so on. Phelan's specialty was munitions, as I recall. So if one unit is in need of a specialist, if they have a shortage in that discipline, they can engineer a trade with another unit that has a different need to be filled, provided that unit would not be rendered deficient in the specialty they are giving up."

"Do you throw in draft choices?"

"I assume that is an unsuccessful attempt at humor? It's late and I am needed elsewhere, Lieutenant."

"Sorry. So Phelan left in a trade?"

"Yes, and he subsequently left the army."

"And once he was traded out, he would

no longer have been in close proximity to Gero?"

"That is almost certainly true, though my memory does not include that. I really had no interest in following Phelan's career."

I'm about to get off the call when something he said earlier takes center stage in my mind. "Major, when we started talking about this, you said that 'they were quite a group.' "

"And?"

"And by group, did you mean the unit itself, or Phelan and Gero? Groups usually have more than two people."

"Yes, they do. I could have said 'trio'; they were a tight-knit, undisciplined group of three."

"Phelan, Gero, and who else?"

"I believe his name was Scanlon. Yes, Scanlon . . . Rodney Scanlon. Are we done here, Lieutenant?"

"We are done." I thank the major and send him back to his dinner; I hope his tablemates appreciate his witty repartee. Then I call back to General Thielen's office to speak with Lieutenant Anderson, who I now consider my military information genie.

I tell him about Scanlon and request any information he can provide, especially any contact information the army may ever have had. He promises to get back to me, and I know he will. Genies are very reliable that way.

I finally get off the phone and turn to Jessie and Nate. They've heard my end of the conversations, so it isn't necessary to say it, but I do anyway.

"There's a chance we've found our number three."

Roderick, not Rodney, Scanlon was born and raised in Fort Smith, Arkansas.

He managed to graduate high school, though his army proficiency reports make it clear that he wasn't exactly a Mensa candidate. He worked in and around Fort Smith for a few years, not doing anything noteworthy, before enlisting.

He seemed to have found himself in the army and, as Major Taggart indicated, he was a talented soldier. He re-upped for three separate tours to Iraq, and it was during the third one that he started to get into trouble with his pair of stablemates, Phelan and Gero. His record includes a number of disciplinary actions for after-hours wrongdoing, mostly bar fights and minor assault charges.

Scanlon left the service almost a year after Phelan transferred out of that unit. He came to the New York/New Jersey area, and we have a residence on file for him on Long Island. The reason that is part of his record is that he went to the local VA hospital for a knee injury suffered in Iraq. That may well be why he went to Long Island in the first place; there's no way for us to know.

All of this information is provided by Lieutenant Anderson. We put Jessie and her team on the case, and they quickly learn that Scanlon no longer lives at the address on Long Island. In fact, that address doesn't exist anymore; it was knocked down to make room for a mall.

Jessie is not worried; she has all of Scanlon's relevant information, including his Social Security number. "If he's on the planet, we'll find him," she says. An hour later she comes back and adds, "He's not just on the planet; he's in New Jersey."

Scanlon's last known address is a garden apartment in Lodi. It's a complex of at least forty furnished apartments, and the address we have for his is near the back. That's good, because we're starting off by talking to the manager, and his office is in the front.

Nate waits outside while I go in by myself. There is a small sign outside the manager's unit, which seems to be just another garden apartment, that identifies him as Jonathan Wynn. So when I knock on the already open door to the office, I say, "Mr. Wynn?"

"Yeah? You looking to rent?"

Apparently, this complex is not quite full. "Actually, I'm just looking for a friend."

"So join Facebook."

"His name is Rod Scanlon."

He almost does a double take on hearing this. "You think you want to find him? Take a number, pal. Your friend is an asshole."

"Why do you say that?"

"Because he stuck me with a month's rent and took off. So unless you're going to make good on it, you can take off too."

Mr. Wynn seems like someone who it's easy to quickly grow tired of. "I don't think this is going to work that way," I say. I go back to the open door and signal for Nate to come in, and then turn back to Wynn. I take out my badge, show it to him, and say, "Let's talk some more about my friend, while my other friend comes in."

"Well, what the hell do you know? He's wanted by the cops? That's a real shocker. What did the prick do?"

"The way this will work, Mr. Wynn, is that we will ask the questions. You can handle the answering part of the conversation. That way everyone has a lane to stay in."

"And what if I don't want to?"

"Then we'll assume it's the environment

that is causing the problem, and we'll reconvene down at the station. In fact, we can all drive down there together. We'll be in the front of the car, and you'll be in the back wearing handcuffs."

"You going to arrest me if I refuse?"

I turn to Nate, and he shrugs and says, "Works for me; I'll get the cuffs out of the car."

Wynn is indignant. "On what charge?"

"Suspicion of being a pain in the ass. Even though you're clearly guilty, you'll probably beat it, but my guess is it will take thirty-six hours, during which time you will be behind bars. That can feel much longer than it actually is, but you can spend the time telling your cellmates how tough you are."

"You guys are unbelievable," he says. "This used to be goddamn America. What do you want to know?"

"Everything you know about Rod Scanlon."

It turns out that he doesn't know that much, or at least that's what he claims. I tend to believe him, since he probably has forty or fifty tenants, and there is no reason to think he has gotten close to them. Wynn does not seem like that friendly a guy.

According to Wynn, Scanlon came and rented the place about two and a half months ago. "I remember when I showed it to him, it was like he didn't care what it looked like. He was like, 'whatever, I'll take it.'"

"Did you see much of him after that?" Nate asks. "Ever see him with any friends?"

"What am I running a social club?" he asks, but when Nate gives him his "I'm going to crush you like a bug" stare, he adds, "I don't notice stuff like that; I give people their privacy. But Scanlon's apartment was near the back, so he wouldn't have come through this entrance. No reason I would see him." He thinks a moment and adds, "He wanted the apartment back there; we've got plenty of them all over. But he wanted that one."

"So he left without paying his rent?"

Wynn nods. "Five weeks."

"You know what kind of car he drove?"

We catch a break in that tenants have to provide Wynn with the make and model of their car, plus the license-plate number. That's how they get a parking space on the premises and don't get towed. He gives us the information; it's a 2014 Kia Optima, metallic green.

Wynn says that Scanlon's apartment has remained empty since he left; there are other vacancies in the complex as well, and they have been empty longer than this one. For that reason he hasn't shown it to anyone yet, and, in fact, hasn't even had it cleaned or done any painting or repairs that might be necessary.

Wynn agrees to show us the apartment; he's more cooperative now. I think he's more afraid of Nate than spending a week-end in jail. I can't say I blame him.

The apartment is bland and depressing, furnished with the kind of stuff you'd find in the cheapest of chain hotels. It's also empty except for those furnishings; there is nothing left of Scanlon's things that I can see.

"We're going to be sending a few cops here to guard this room until our forensic people have a chance to go over it," I say. "I assume that won't be a problem?"

"You going to pay me rent?" Wynn asks.

"No. We're going to rely on you being a civic-minded citizen."

Rod Scanlon expected the next four days to be the longest of his life.

He had spent the last two weeks holed up in a dump of a hotel room, completely cut off and only getting his news from television. The garden apartment he had left was the Ritz-Carlton compared to this place.

He was stunned to find out through news reports that Gero was dead, and yet he had not heard a word about Phelan or anyone else. This was by design; the conspirators had said that they would not be in communication at all, so as to reduce and hopefully eliminate the chance of detection.

Still, just the idea of Gero's death had a major impact on him. Not so much because they went back a long time together, though Gero was as close as anyone to being what Scanlon would call a buddy. No, the reason he was so struck by Gero's death was that none of the conspirators were supposed to die. They were all destined to live long, very wealthy lives.

Other people were supposed to be the only ones who died.

Scanlon had one job to do, and one job only: To make sure that the operation ended in a blaze of glory — or, more accurately, a burst of glory. He knew the plan was foolproof provided he was not detected in advance, which meant the next four days would be spent right where he was.

Once that mission was accomplished, he could disappear and start collecting more money than he ever imagined. All of that was prearranged and foolproof, but it all depended on him.

He would succeed; there was no doubt about that. But the waiting would be torture.

The phone ringing in the silent room was jarring. Scanlon actually jumped, a sign that his nerves were on edge.

The voice on the other end did not mention Gero. The message was short and to the point, and it implicitly reflected the fact that Gero was no longer available.

Scanlon had another job to do.

His responsibilities had expanded.

We have absolutely no evidence against Scanlon, circumstantial or otherwise.

At the moment there is nothing to tie him to whatever crime conspiracy Phelan and Gero were involved in. Should we be able to find him, all we could do would be to question him, listen to his denials, and send him on his way.

But even though prosecutors and grand juries, by law, cannot weigh gut feelings, we've got plenty of those. Nate and I both have strong cop instincts that Scanlon is deeply involved in this.

They were the closest of buddies in the army, often operating at least marginally outside the law. That in itself is not incriminating; a close high school buddy of mine is currently serving time for running a financial Ponzi scheme, but I wouldn't know Ponzi if I ran into him in a supermarket.

The fact that Scanlon has recently disappeared, or at least run out on his apartment, is suspicious as well. It was more or less timed to the outbreak of murders; Scanlon could have played a role in them, or he could just have been escaping the increasing pressure.

But even the location of that apartment is curious. Here was a guy born in Arkansas, who served in various overseas locations, who winds up settling in Lodi, New Jersey, despite having no job, family, or other ties that we can locate.

I have nothing against Lodi; it's a fine place. But in the absence of any apparent benign reason, why move there? It's not South Beach, or Vegas, or Palm Springs. Nobody buys a time-share in Lodi, New Jersey. So why take an apartment there, only to bail out weeks later?

I also found it significant that Wynn described Scanlon as basically uninterested in the specifics of the apartment itself, other than wanting it to be located in the back of the complex. It sounds like somebody who wanted to hide, possibly biding his time, without being noticed.

Hovering over all of this is motive. What seemed to be random, deranged killings over ridiculously small grudges, real or perceived, has morphed into something bigger.

Phelan could have crossed over into an unbalanced state in which he committed heinous acts in what was basically a fit of pique. But to have brought Gero along, and maybe Scanlon, just doesn't make logical sense. And the more people that are involved, the less sense it makes.

Criminal motives almost always come down to either sex, power, or money, not necessarily in that order, and sometimes a combination of two or all three. Yet none of them seem to apply here. There is no indication whatsoever of any sexual motives; the victims do not seem to have any relationship of any meaningful kind with their killers, and they certainly were not molested.

There could be a power motive, if you consider the feeling of power involved in controlling life and death. But again, the apparent involvement of three people weighs against that, and for all we know there could be more than three.

That leaves money. But there's no indication yet that the killers have profited from their actions. We've talked to the families of the victims, and there's been no mention of any outsiders invading the estates and laying claim to the money. Additionally, while

Brookings and Randowsky were probably well-off financially, the other victims included a retired school teacher, a bellman, a gas station attendant, and a librarian. Possibly they had money independent of their work, we can find that out, but as a group they were not exactly Fortune 500 CEOs.

"Could it somehow be insurance?" I say it out loud without really meaning to, and Nate hears me.

"Could what be insurance?" he asks — a perfectly reasonable question.

"Could they be taking insurance policies out on these people, and then cashing in when they've killed them?"

I don't wait for an answer because Nate has no more way of knowing than I do. Instead I call Jessie and ask her to come in.

When she does, I say, "You said that Helen Mizell left three insurance policies. Two were for her kids, and one small one for some woman that you hadn't found."

She nods. "Right. Marcia Carnow."

"Have you found her?"

"I don't think so, but I'll check with Roger; I think I assigned it to him. But we've had other priorities, and this didn't seem terribly important."

"It might be," I say, and then explain my theory. Actually, calling it a "theory" is probably giving it too much credit.

"The policy was for fifty thousand dollars," she points out. "Assuming they somehow got the money from this Marcia Carnow, or if Marcia Carnow were a co-conspirator, at that pace it would still take a long time to get rich."

I nod. "I know. But let's track this woman down and talk to her. And let's find out if these other victims carried suspicious life insurance policies. Maybe we'll get a hit."

She nods. "Worth trying. We'll get right on it."

Sergeant Tony Arguello calls and says, "Doug, you might want to get down here."

"Where are you?"

"Scanlon's apartment. There's something you should see."

I don't bother asking what it is; I've learned that someone like Arguello will not waste my time, so I just head down there knowing it's important. Nate has a mountain of paperwork to go through, so he stays behind with my promise to call him if needed.

When I arrive at the complex I go in through the back, which is where Scanlon had wanted his apartment. I see Arguello's van and another cop car; they've been stationed here to guard the place until we are finished with it.

I go inside and see Tony and one of his people in the small kitchen, sitting at what looks like a bridge table, but which is the only table in the room. When we were here, I assumed that was where Scanlon had eaten his meals. Based on all the gear that Tony is using to examine the table, I've got a feeling he's not having a pizza.

Tony looks up and sees me come in, waving me over.

"What've you got?" I ask.

He points to a microscope on the table. "Take a look."

I do so, and still have no idea what he's talking about. "Tony, all I see is an enlarged piece of table."

"Okay, it doesn't matter. I've tested it, and it's positive for RDX. We'll do more definitive tests back at the lab, but I think it will show the same thing. We rarely get false positives for RDX."

"What is RDX?"

"It's a chemical used to make explosives. It's used in combination with other chemicals that help to insure its stability, but it's extraordinarily powerful."

"How powerful?" I ask.

"You ever see those videos where they bring down old stadiums or huge buildings?

That's RDX."

"Shit," is my one-word answer, and I take out my phone and call Nate. When he answers, I say, "Take a look at the army records on Scanlon we got from Lieutenant Anderson."

A few moments later, Nate says, "Got 'em. What do you want to know?"

"Somewhere on there it should say his specialty. Do you see it?"

"Hold on." I wait for at least two or three minutes until he finally comes back on the line.

"Here it is," he says. "Specialty is munitions."

"Damn." Major Taggart had said that the unit would have been willing to trade a munitions specialist like Phelan only if they were covered — meaning they already had another such specialist. They did: Scanlon.

I inform Tony that we are going to have to alert the FBI to this new information. I'm sure they will bring in homeland security, but we will continue to work independent of them.

Rod Scanlon wanted an apartment in the back of the complex and didn't care how livable and comfortable it was because he was using it as a bomb factory.

The phone rings at six o'clock in the morning.

That's rarely a good time for a phone to ring, but in some cases it could be okay. If it rings in an all-night diner, or a dairy farm, there might be no problem. When it's a homicide detective's home phone, it's downright ominous.

I force myself to pick up the phone and it's the desk sergeant. "There's been a shooting," he says. "In Ridgewood."

"Who got shot?"

"Actually, no one. They missed."

"Good. Sergeant, I'm a homicide detective, not an attempted-homicide detective. Call someone else and then throw away this number."

"It appears to be related to your case," he says. "Bradley had me call you."

"Did you speak to Nate?"

"Done. He's going out to the scene."

The sergeant gives me the details. The intended victim is Evan Meyer, Phelan's ex-boss at the trucking company. He was apparently leaving his house at five thirty to go to his office; I remember he had mentioned to me that he always gets to work by six.

The potential killer may have known this routine, because he tried a drive-by shooting when Meyer left the house and was heading for his car.

Meyer is not going to make it into work this morning; he's at his house, and Nate and I are heading there as well.

Nate is in the kitchen with Meyer when I arrive. Cops are outside guarding the scene, and forensics is working in the driveway. As soon as I walk in, Meyer recognizes me and says, "It's you; I should have known. Who took a shot at me?"

"Maybe you can tell me that," I say, and then I look at Nate. He shrugs and says, "I just got here. We can hear the story together."

"First of all, Mr. Meyer, are you okay? Are you injured?"

"No, the son of a bitch missed me."

"Please tell us what happened, starting at the beginning, and include every detail you can remember."

"That won't take long," he says. "I walked out my front door to my car, which was parked in the driveway. As I was doing it, I saw a car about three houses down. It started moving even though I didn't hear it start up, so it had to have been running.

"It just seemed strange. It was going west, which means he should have been on the other side of the street, but he wasn't. He was on my side. He had his left hand up, like he was concealing his face. Then I saw him raise his other arm, and there was something in his hand.

"I was in the army, you know? So I had this feeling . . . I dove to the ground, and as I did, I heard the shot. I don't know what it hit, maybe the garage, but I crawled under the car. I was able to see the street from there, and he was gone. Son of a bitch is a real profile in courage."

"Did you get a look at him?" Nate asks.

"Not a great one. I doubt I could identify him."

"What about the car?"

"I'm good with cars; this was one of those Korean ones. A Kia."

"Color?"

"Like a metallic green."

He's describing Scanlon's car. It's not proof that Scanlon is involved, not by a long

272

shot, but it's certainly contributing evidence.

"We'll be sending someone out with some photographs for you to look at, to see if you can make an identification."

"I can't."

"You never know," Nate says. "It will be helpful if you try."

He nods. "Okay." Then, "That wasn't Phelan who shot at me. I would have recognized him."

"Can you think of any reason he would have wanted to?"

"No. He walked out on me; I didn't fire him. I still have his last check; he didn't wait for it. But all he'd have to do is ask me for it, so that couldn't be it."

"Can you think of anyone who might want to cause you this kind of harm?"

"No. Definitely not, that I know of."

"Does the name Rod Scanlon mean anything to you?"

He thinks for a moment. "No, not that I can recall. But I may not be thinking too clearly right now."

I nod. "Understood. We'll be sending someone to show you the photographs. Will you be here this morning?"

"Oh, yeah. Today I work from home."

On its face, the attempted murder of Evan Meyer seems part of an established pattern.

It was a shooting without warning and without apparent motive of a person who has some connection to Danny Phelan. Knowing what the grudge might be is not important. If Phelan had a reason to be angry at his high school English teacher from twenty-five years ago, he certainly could hold some grievance toward his boss.

But somehow this feels different. For one thing, the shot missed. That simply has not happened before. It could certainly be explained by a different shooter; Gero probably did the dirty work before, and with his death, someone else has stepped in.

The leader in the clubhouse for most-likely shooter, at least at this point, is Rod Scanlon. Maybe he is just not as accurate a marksman as Gero. We already know that his specialty is munitions, not marksmanship. Also, he was shooting from a moving car, which represents a definite change in MO.

This shooting also feels too "on the money." Until now, the connection between Phelan and his victims, with the notable exception of his ex-wife, has seemed obscure. In some of the cases we don't even know that link yet. But the attack on Meyer leaves no room for subtlety; who among us hasn't wanted to take a shot at their boss at some point? Barely a day goes by that I don't consider doing a drive-by on Captain Bradley.

Still, we are dealing with people who until this point have not made a mistake, not even a hint of one. This attempt feels more haphazard, more seat of the pants. With careful planning Meyer could easily have been taken down, but he wasn't. He saw them coming from a mile, or at least a few houses, away, and he was able to take evasive action without much difficulty.

I verbalize all of this to Nate, and he surprises me with, "Maybe it was meant to fail."

"What do you mean?"

"Maybe Meyer is in on it. Maybe he's the damn ringleader. He was Phelan's boss before, so maybe he still is. He was in the army, right? Maybe he was part of this group back then. They take a shot at him and deliberately miss so we think it can't be him because they tried to kill him. But maybe they want us to think that."

"But we've never suspected Meyer," I say.

"They have no way of knowing that."

"You really believe this, Nate?"

"Nope. Not a chance. Just talking out loud."

I nod. "Next time you talk out loud, try and do it when you're alone, or maybe put a pillow over your face."

"Or maybe I could stuff the pillow down your throat," he says. Then, "You don't think it's possible?"

"I doubt it, but let's pull Meyer's army records just in case. At this point I think the only army records we haven't seen are George Patton's."

Captain Bradley comes in. He's just finished giving another public update on the situation, this time adding Julie Phelan and Rod Scanlon to the list of "persons of interest" he wants the public to watch for.

Our tip lines have already been overrun by citizens making reports of sightings, none of which have worked out. Although the truth is, we have not been able to run down all of them; there are just too many.

Generally big media stories explode and then slowly peter out. The length of time it takes for them to run their course depends on the impact of the story, and the subsequent events that give it renewed life. In this case there has been no lessening of interest at all, and more shootings and more "persons of interest" provide it with ongoing oxygen.

"Talk to me about Evan Meyer," Bradley says when he enters the office. He knew about the shooting before I did. But he's been with the commissioner all morning before the press conference and hasn't been updated.

Nate takes him through the events of this morning, leaving out the theory that Meyer arranged the shooting himself, to cover his guilt.

"So what's the assumption here?" Bradley asks when Nate is finished.

"That Gero was the previous shooter, and now that Doc Holliday here took him out, it's Scanlon. Scanlon just isn't as good at it as Gero."

"Could it have been Phelan?" Bradley asks.

I shake my head. "Meyer said he would have recognized Phelan."

Bradley nods and updates us on what he

has learned from the commissioner about the FBI involvement. So far they seem to be making very little progress beyond developing psychological profiles on Danny and Julia Phelan.

"What's their view on Julie?" I ask.

"They think she's at least an accessory," he says. "A lot of psychological horseshit, but at the end of the day they think she's under her father's spell. I told them about Scanlon, so I'm sure another profile is coming."

"And what about Scanlon?"

"I don't know," he says, "But their level of interest sure went up when that explosive was found in his apartment."

Jessie comes in to join the club, but by the look on her face, my guess is she hasn't solved the crime. "I have a little strange news and a lot of bad. Which do you want first?"

I would opt for bad, but Bradley chooses strange.

"We've been checking into life insurance policies on the victims," she says. "The strange one is Helen Mizell. We can't find the third beneficiary, besides the two sons. Her name is Marcia Carnow, and it was just fifty thousand."

"Why can't you find her?" I ask.

She shrugs. "I don't know. Maybe she was using an assumed name, but there is no Marcia Carnow that fits the circumstances. The address given was bogus."

"Can you follow the money?" Bradley asks.

"Not so far. An account was opened and then closed, apparently only to receive this money. Then it was wired to an offshore account; we can't trace it."

"So what do you make of it?" Bradley asks.

"No way to tell, obviously. Could be we're just not seeing something that's right in front of us. There's just no one else to ask."

"This whole thing can't be about fifty thousand dollars," I say. Then, "That's the strange news; what's the bad?"

"There are no similar situations among the other victims. Most of them had life insurance policies; in fact, they all did except for Decker, the gas station owner. But every one checks out; they all had spouses or kids as beneficiaries. Nothing suspicious, and only Brookings and Randowsky had policies for substantial amounts. I don't think this is the answer," Jessie says.

Another unproductive meeting breaks up, leaving me disappointed that my insurance idea, even though I knew it was a longshot, didn't pan out. Phelan, Scanlon, and the now-deceased Gero have to be getting something out of this, but we're not getting any closer to finding out what that is.

The phone rings, and I can immediately hear the anxiety in James McKinney's voice. He gets right to the point.

"Julie called me."

Rather than conduct the conversation on the phone, Nate and I go to McKinney's house.

At this point, a call from Julie Phelan qualifies as a major development, and we're going to want to go over every detail carefully.

When we arrive and knock on the door, McKinney opens it without exposing himself to anyone outside; he stands behind the door to shield himself. This is one scared, careful guy.

He had said he was going to hide after hearing that Phelan threatened him personally. I thought he meant he would leave his home, and that's the first thing I ask him about.

"I stayed in a hotel for a couple of days, but it was near here and didn't feel any safer," he says. "So I came here to get some things, and now I'm leaving for a good long time."

"Where are you going?"

"I'm not going to share that information with you."

"Why not?"

"Because I can't trust it won't get in the wrong hands. I'm sorry, Lieutenant, and this is nothing against you personally, but do you realize what happened the last time? I told you that Phelan might be in the cabin, and the next thing I know he's threatening me for turning on him. Somehow he found out that I spoke to you."

"Maybe Julie told him."

"Julie didn't know."

"When did Julie call you this time?"

"Right before I called you. So just like forty-five minutes ago."

"What did she say?"

"That I had to trust her, that she was going to do what was right. She sounded scared, almost panicked."

"What else?"

"She said that something terrible was going to happen if she didn't stop it. She said she didn't know what it was yet, but her father said that 'all of them would pay.' Then she said she had to get off the phone, but that I should trust her. I had the feeling that she heard someone coming and couldn't talk."

"Were there any background noises? Anything that might help identify where she was?" Nate asks.

McKinney thinks for a few moments. "You know, I think so . . . yeah. It made it a little hard to hear her. It sounded like there were cars going by, like she was on a highway or something."

"Anything else?"

"No, not that I can remember. I wasn't thinking too clearly; she sounded like she was in over her head on this, like she was trying to stay in control of something but couldn't do it. She doesn't deserve this."

"What phone did she call you on?" I ask.

"My cell phone."

"Did your caller ID show you what phone she was on? Was it hers?"

"It said 'Unknown Caller,' so it couldn't have been hers. Hers comes through with her name on it."

"We need to examine your phone records to determine where the call came from. We can get a warrant, but it would be faster if you would authorize it now."

"Of course. Absolutely. Whatever you need, and whatever gets us beyond this. But I'm out of here. I'll be back when I see

Phelan in handcuffs or worse on television. And maybe not even then."

He gives us the cell number that received the call and signs a note authorizing complete access. We could obviously get the information without it, but it will save us a couple of hours, and hours could be important if Julie's warning is right and something big is going to happen.

Nate and I ask him a bunch more questions, but he has no more answers. He seems to calm down some as we talk, but clearly the stress of it all is getting to him. He mentions a few times that he "didn't sign on for this." I think all of this may be having an effect on the idyllic relationship; fear has a tendency to do that.

As we're about to leave, I tell him to be careful.

"Oh, I will," he says. "This is embarrassing . . . but I bought it online."

With that he opens a couple of buttons of his shirt, revealing a bulletproof vest under it. "I don't know if it would work, and I sure hope I don't find out, but it makes me feel better. I'm just glad no one in the office has seen it; they'd mock the hell out of me."

"Looks pretty solid," Nate says. "What kind of work do you do?"

"I'm a broker."

Nate points to me. "You should talk to him; he's got all the money."

McKinney's recounting of the conversation with Julie puts her role in question.

We've been operating under the assumption that Julie is neck deep into the conspiracy with her father. It seemed that, even though she may not have been in it from the beginning, she at least moved to the point where she was abetting it.

We believed this because of the note in the cabin that Phelan left when he committed the murder. In it he threatened McKinney, in effect vowing revenge for McKinney going to the police and revealing his whereabouts at the cabin. The only way that Phelan could have known that McKinney was talking to us is if Julie told him.

But there is always the possibility that Julie had become her father's prisoner and had no choice but to tell him about McKinney. It seems less logical than our original theory, but the recent call supports it.

Like everything else in this frustrating case, it could go either way. And bottom line: it doesn't matter. We are doing our best to find Julie, and once we have, we'll figure out where she stands.

Jessie comes in to update Nate and me on the check into McKinney's phone records. The call from Julie to him lasted thirty-two seconds, a time which is consistent with his recounting of the content.

"It's from a burner phone," Jessie says. "Purchased almost two months ago from a 7–Eleven in Elmwood Park. Paid for in cash."

"Obviously Phelan was planning ahead," Nate says.

"Was there a GPS in it?" Almost all phones have GPS signals which the phone company can use to locate it. The only exceptions are certain primitive burner phones.

Jessie nods. "There was. The call was made from a rest stop off of Route 80, near Parsippany."

"So they're on the move," Nate says.

Jessie nods. "They might be, but the phone isn't. It's still there. They must have thrown it away after she made the call."

So "there" is where Nate and I go. It's about a twenty-five-minute drive, and according to Jessie's reading of satellite photos, the rest area is in a secluded, wooded area.

My hope is that we find the phone; my fear is that we're going to find a body along with it. There is always the possibility that Phelan discovered Julie making the call and killed her for it. Knowing that she made the call would be a clear reason for discarding the phone; if he were savvy enough to buy a burner phone in advance, he would likely have known that a phone GPS can be tracked.

It doesn't make sense that she would have discarded the phone after using it. If she really is trying to stop what her father is doing, then she has no reason to avoid detection.

On the way, Nate calls and requests that four other officers meet us at the rest stop. The phone might not be easy to locate; if it were, it would probably have been found and taken by someone else. And while it is still giving off GPS signals, that might end soon. Once the battery runs out, the phone will no longer be able to be seen by the satellite towers.

Nate and I arrive first. There is a small

building which includes men's and women's bathrooms, with vending machines outside. Two cars are in the small parking lot; a man and woman are in the front seat of one, about to drive away.

Nate goes over to them to make sure they didn't find the phone, while I look to see if there are any security cameras in the area. Once I determine that there aren't, I go into the men's room to see if I can find at least one of the people from the remaining car.

The open doorway leads to a hall that bends around a corridor into the restroom. A stall door opens and a guy, probably fifty years old, comes out and sees me, reacting with surprise. He hadn't heard me come in because there had been no sound of a door opening and closing.

"I didn't —" he starts, but doesn't finish.

"State police," I say, and based on his reaction, I have turned his surprise into shock. It's lucky he's finished in the stall, this experience will probably keep him constipated for a week. He seems so scared that I half expect someone else to come out of the stall after him.

"What's the matter? I . . ."

"I need to know if you found a missing phone, here at the rest stop."

"No, I . . ."

He hasn't finished a sentence yet, but the ones he's started haven't been too promising. "Thank you," I say, and leave. He follows me out and gets in his car, driving off. There must not be anyone in the women's restroom; either that or he left her behind, since there are no cars remaining.

Nate and I start to search for the phone; there aren't that many places it could be. When we don't find it in the immediate area, we expand our search to the wooded area near the parking lot. Within five minutes, Nate finds it on the ground. It has 4 percent remaining in the battery.

We search the same area for any other evidence that can be of value, like maybe a map showing exactly where they were going, or a signed confession. We don't find either.

The cops that we called to the scene are no longer needed, so when they show up a minute later, we send them away. Nate carefully places the phone in an evidence bag, and we head back to the station.

"He must have caught her with it," Nate says. "Why else would he throw it away?"

I can't think of any other reason. He'd be worried we could trace it, so he got rid of it. It also cements the idea that Julie is not there of her own free will, and might well be in significant danger. Phelan does not seem to be the sentimental-father type.

The forensics people come in to check for prints on the phone and run them for identification. It doesn't take long, mainly because there is no running necessary. The phone has been wiped clean of prints.

"Why the hell would he bother to do that?" Nate asks. I'm not keeping an exact count, but that probably makes three thousand questions about this case that I can't answer. So Nate continues, "The only way anyone who found that phone would check the prints is if we got it, and he'd be aware we already know whose phone it is. Any passerby who found it is not going to dust it for prints."

"At least we didn't find a body," I say. "And it now seems more likely that Julie is not part of this. She clearly made the call in secret, though Phelan found out. She wouldn't have done that if they were partners."

All that is left for us to do is send cops to check if Phelan got gas east or west of the rest stop, or if they stopped to eat. Even if we get lucky, we'll only learn which direction they were going — but then again, you never know.

In this case, we unfortunately know. Our

Rod Scanlon was freaking out.

He had just watched on television as some state police captain identified him and Julie Phelan as persons of interest in the hunt for the killers. That flew in the face of everything that he had been promised, and was of such huge significance that he needed time to process it.

An absolute guarantee of anonymity is the reason he signed on, that and the obvious lure of becoming wealthier than he had ever imagined. He initially had just one job to do, and though it was the climactic and most important job of all, it would be easy to accomplish.

Then Gero was killed, which in itself was scary enough. Gero was as tough and ruthless a guy as there was on the planet, there were a lot of Iraqi terrorists who could attest to that. But he went down, and Scanlon reluctantly filled in when called upon.

He took the shot at Meyer, Phelan's boss. But Scanlon felt there was no way the cops could have made him as the shooter; he was in and out of there quickly, and there were no pain-in-the-ass neighbors around. Meyer could not have gotten a good look at him; he was sure of that.

But the cops sure as hell knew about him; there was his face on goddamn television. Of course, that face had changed somewhat; he now had a beard and was wearing glasses, just in case of an eventuality like this. Their photograph obviously did not reflect those changes.

He was only going to have to go out once more, and then he would disappear, so he wasn't so worried about being seen in the short term. But what about the rest of his life? Are the arrangements foolproof? Apparently not, if Gero went down.

But he kept going back to the question: How could the cops know about him? Could they have guessed it, just because he and Gero and Phelan were buddies in the army? That was certainly a possibility; once Gero went down, then they would look for connections to Phelan. Scanlon figured his name could have come up then.

He briefly considered turning himself in. Except for firing the shot at Meyer, he hadn't committed a crime. He could go to the cops and tell them everything he knew in return for lenient treatment. He might even avoid prison time.

But then he wouldn't get the money. The money was what it was all about; he just simply wanted to live life as a rich person. Working a job, or punching a clock, or struggling to pay the rent . . . that was not the way Scanlon wanted to live.

But the rules had changed. He wasn't going to be stranded on this island, not knowing what was going on. And he was not going to take on all of this new difficulty without being compensated for it.

So he would go after the money; he would do his job.

But then he would get some answers.

The thing about explosives that not many people understand is that they're not dangerous.

That is to say that most of the individual chemicals and compounds that make them up are not dangerous, until and unless they are combined in specific ways.

That is why they often can be purchased without any real scrutiny. Each of the ingredients has other, harmless uses, so there is no need to regulate them. If someone came in and asked for TNT, that would be noticed because it's licensed and regulated. But fertilizer, as one example, can be used in explosives or to grow corn.

To further make the point, you can use a scissors to stab someone to death, but scissors have other functions, therefore sales of scissors are neither regulated nor prohibited. So it is with the chemicals in the bomb that our experts think Scanlon was making.

We've sent a bunch of cops out to all relevant retail stores within fifty miles to show Scanlon's picture and try to identify any purchases he might have made. It is no surprise that they've learned nothing. A search of credit card records also comes up empty; if Scanlon made such purchases, he either used a fake name or paid in cash.

We've also put a tap on McKinney's phone. I'm sure this required a bit of maneuvering with the judge, since McKinney is not under suspicion. But the nature of the situation, with the prospect of many more killings, must have put irresistible pressure on that judge. Fortunately, McKinney had signed over permission for us to access his phone records, and I had deliberately written up that authorization in a wide, all-inclusive manner. I suspect that was a significant factor in getting the judge to sign off on the tap.

We're interested in McKinney's phone for a few reasons. First of all, we want to be able to find him if we need him. He's going into hiding, which is all well and good, but we don't want him hiding from us.

More importantly, if he gets another call from Julie, we want to know it in the moment. We can't afford to wait for him to report the call, or decide not to. We want the number it comes from, in order to trace the GPS location if possible.

We also want to know what is said on any such call. McKinney is compromised by his feelings toward Julie, and while we don't currently consider it likely that she is complicit in her father's crimes, she could say something that McKinney might not want to promptly relay to us, if at all. We want to know the content of the calls firsthand.

It's an invasion of McKinney's privacy, but the truth is that I'm more concerned about the damage that can be done by Scanlon's explosive.

Right now, for all our efforts, we're in the same reactive mode we've been in since this started. Phelan does something, either an act of violence or sending a note, and we scurry around trying to use it to our advantage. We haven't successfully done that yet, and I've got a feeling that time is running short.

Nate and I constantly remind each other that we need to avoid getting caught in the weeds and must instead focus on the big picture, the one key that might unlock this thing.

"For me it's still motive," Nate says. "I just don't buy the grudge crap. Maybe Phelan turned nut job, that's one thing, but

I don't see Gero and Scanlon going along for his ride."

I nod. "I agree. But they wanted us to think it was about Phelan's grudges. And don't forget, we weren't supposed to know about Gero and Scanlon. It's not about sex or power, so it has to be about money."

"What if it is all about one or two victims?" Nate asks. "Maybe they figured out a way to get big money from one or two of the estates, and the rest of the killings have just been cover for that, so we won't know where to look."

"It's possible, but the only two victims with any real money have been Brookings and Randowsky, and we've seen no evidence that their deaths have been a financial boon to anyone. Plus, they were well off, but they weren't Warren Buffett."

"Then maybe the key killing hasn't happened yet," he says.

It's a good point, but before I have a chance to respond, I get a call from our local postmaster, Sandy Geary. She's been alerted to contact me if anything comes in resembling the notes that we have received so far. We don't want to wait until it's sent out for delivery with the regular mail, so we've asked her to monitor our incoming mail and flag anything suspicious.

"I'm pretty sure we got one," she says.

"Thanks; I'll send someone out to pick it up."

I send a squad car out to get it, and they bring along a forensics cop to make sure it's handled carefully. They are back within a half hour, and Nate and I are there when it's opened.

It says:

"Any day now . . . BOOM!"

It could not have gone easier.

Rod Scanlon left his motel room at around twelve thirty in the afternoon. He didn't have to put the "do not disturb" sign on the door, it had essentially been there since he moved in. And it had come in handy, because Rod Scanlon definitely did not want to be disturbed, and the hotel chambermaid had been respectful of that.

He had pulled up in the van in the back of the restaurant. It was by then one o'clock, at the height of the lunch hour, so the entire waitstaff was in the front restaurant section, dealing with the packed dining room.

Scanlon unloaded the cooking materials, the pans and serving dishes ubiquitous at catered events. He brought them in through the open back door, attracting absolutely no attention in the process. What he was doing looked completely normal for the time and location.

Only one person even saw him, a kitchen worker who never in a million years would have stopped to wonder why he was bringing such materials into a restaurant storage area already well-stocked with them.

Scanlon went to a storage closet packed with everything from spare napkins to tablecloths to pots to cleaning supplies. It was all extra stuff and had the look of material that had not been used or needed for a very long time.

He carefully placed the device, contained in an opaque plastic container, on a back shelf. The possibility it might be discovered in the next thirty-six hours was so remote as to not even be a consideration. The phone was already set in place, but he also set the timer, so that a phone call would not be necessary and would only be a backup if the timer for some reason didn't work.

Scanlon knew that would not be necessary; the timer would work. He was a pro.

Then he gathered up the excess materials and went back out the rear door, the same way he had come in. The entire process took no more than five minutes, without so much as a single tense moment.

Just before he got back in the van, he remembered to check his phone to make sure that there was sufficient cell service for the device. He had checked it before, but he was a careful man, so he was just confirming that the coverage had not changed.

He had full service . . . four bars, which meant the phone on the device had four bars, since it was the same provider.

At that point only two things could go wrong. The cell tower could have an outage, or somebody could dial the number on the device unintentionally — a wrong number. Both were extremely unlikely, and very worth the risk.

Scanlon was a bit nervous being out and about; that's what happens when your photograph is all over television as being a "person of interest" in a serial-killer case. But he felt he had altered his appearance well enough to escape detection by a casual observer, as long as he didn't stay out long and interact with people.

Fortunately, he wasn't going back to that dingy hotel, at least not for a while.

He was going to get answers.

Now.

Alegro Perales spoke excellent English, when she wanted to.

Alegro was a chambermaid at the Village Motel in Garfield, where rooms could be had for thirty dollars a night. A two-story motel with rooms that could only be accessed from outside, it is fair to say that this was not a popular vacation destination, especially in winter.

Alegro had worked there for two years. It was drudge work, but not too difficult, and she needed the money. Alegro and her husband each worked two jobs and were actually managing to save toward the day when they could have a child and be confident of having the financial wherewithal to provide for him or her.

Alegro was born in Glen Rock, about twenty minutes from where she worked. Her parents spoke both Spanish and English in their home, so she was fluent in both. But as a product of the Glen Rock school system, she felt considerably more comfortable speaking English.

Having said that, there were times at work when her Spanish fluency came in very handy. Most of the hotel guests were nice enough; they weren't big tippers, but they smiled at Alegro, made some small talk, and were generally respectful. To these people she spoke English exclusively.

But some of the guests made her nervous, ranging from a little uncomfortable all the way to creeping her out. She made sure she was never alone with those guests in their room; she relied on her instincts to tell her who to avoid. And to them she spoke Spanish, pretending not to understand English at all. It was just easier to avoid them that way, and especially to ignore their often-crude suggestions.

She'd come home and discuss some of those people with her husband, Orestes. He would caution her to be careful around them and not to put herself in any vulnerable position. These cautions were never necessary; Alegro was smart and savvy and could take care of herself.

But suddenly, she was scared. She was watching television and they were showing a photograph of one of those guests who had frightened her. He had never said more than a few words to her, and nothing threatening, but his manner and the way he carried himself had given her chills.

She had only spoken Spanish to him, and a very few words at that. He had been there for two weeks, and had repeatedly declined to let her in to his room to clean up and make the bed. She brought him fresh towels, but he took them at the door.

His name was Carl Todd, but the newsman on television wasn't calling him that. He was calling him Rod Scanlon and saying that he might be involved in the terrible killings that were taking place. He now had a small beard and darker hair, but she was sure that Carl Todd and Rod Scanlon were the same person.

The newsman was saying that it was important for anyone with knowledge of this man to call the police, and they gave the number.

So Alegro and Orestes talked it out. He asked if she was sure that this was the man, and she said that she was positive. He told her that if she was wrong, and it came out that she made the report, her boss might fire her.

"But if I don't call, and he is the man, and if he goes on killing . . ."

She didn't finish the sentence; she didn't have to.

Orestes handed her the phone, and she dialed the number.

Two officers arrived two hours later to hear what she had to say. She told them what she had told Orestes, and she identified photographs that they showed her, picking Scanlon out from an array of other people.

She asked them not to reveal she had been the one to come forward, that she feared for her job and possible retribution by Scanlon if he found out. They said that they would do their best, but could make no promises. They also told her that she might be contacted again.

Within thirty minutes from the time the cops left her apartment, their report was on Doug Brock's desk, with a stamp on it.

It said: "Priority."

The choice of hiding place for Phelan was nothing short of brilliant.

There is nothing more deserted than a summer camp after the camp season has ended. This was a day camp on Lake Hopatcong, and staying there left almost no chance of discovery.

There were six buildings on the camp grounds. Even someone visiting, and there was almost no danger of that happening, would never have any reason to go to the farthest building in the back.

The place was eerily quiet. There was an emptied swimming pool, two tennis courts with the nets taken down, a ragged ballfield, and what looked to be a small parklike playground. Probably noisy with laughter in the summer, but deadly silent now.

All in all, it was the perfect place to hide.

Scanlon was not supposed to be here; he and Gero had been told not to assemble until the operation was over. But now Gero was dead, and Scanlon wanted to know why his name was out in the media.

He had been promised both anonymity and a great deal of money. Now that the anonymity was gone, the money needed to be increased. He was here to make sure that was understood.

He went straight to the building in the back, which for all intents and purposes looked abandoned. He knew better. He knocked to be polite, but he didn't wait for an invitation; he just opened the door.

"Hello, Phelan" were the last two words he would ever say.

We've decided to do this directly, decisively, and violently.

Alegro Perales had passed the photograph test of identifying Scanlon with flying colors, and her description of his behavior perfectly fit what his actions would be like if he was a fugitive.

Perales is a bright, credible witness who comes across as believable, but without anything apparent to gain from coming forward. In fact, she is afraid, an appropriate reaction, and she has told her story reluctantly.

When she added the fact that he had a fairly heavy Southern accent, that clinched it in my mind. Scanlon was born and raised in Arkansas. Maybe Perales is wrong, that's quite possible, but I'm betting against it.

We've gotten the warrant to enter the hotel room; that was the easy part. Normally we would go to the manager, announce our presence, and maybe plan out a diversion, possibly a pretense to get Scanlon to let us into the room.

That's not happening today.

His room is in the corner in the back, allowing us to approach from the sides without being seen. And once we get in place, we are not going to knock on the door. We are going to knock it down or shoot it open, and come in with force. Shock and awe, motel style.

Ms. Perales said that Scanlon is always in the room; she has never seen him even go out for food. So we are operating under the assumption that he will be there, and we are in take-no-prisoners mode, even though the actual goal — our first choice — is to take a prisoner.

The SWAT team is once again in charge. Nate goes to see the hotel manager, not to get his permission or his cooperation, but rather to make sure that he doesn't misunderstand what's happening and attempt to intervene.

My role is to take a position across the parking lot with a pair of binoculars. Once the team is in place, I wait until I confirm that there are no other people in harm's way — no other guests, motel personnel, etc. Then I will electronically notify the SWAT team leader, Lieutenant Morrow, that it's time to move.

Unfortunately, that doesn't happen right away. The couple next door leaves their room, goes down to their car, and then apparently realizes they forgot something in the room. The guy goes back, and it takes a couple of minutes for him to come back out while the woman waits in the car.

Finally, after five minutes that seem like fifty, they drive off, and I signal that the coast is clear. There is no reason to leave where I am; in fact, if I see anything come up that looks like a reason to abort, I can direct them to do so. Not that there is going to be a lot of time; once they move it will be over quickly.

And it is. I watch as they descend on the room, knock the door in, and rush inside. I can hear the screams from where I am; the yelling and loud noise is designed to stun anyone inside.

I don't hear any gunshots, which is a very good thing. Unless it means that Scanlon is not there, which would be a bad thing. We've been down this road before.

I run toward the motel and take the steps two at a time. There's not much noise at all coming out of the room, though some other people have come out of their rooms to see what all the commotion was about. We've already assigned cops to keep bystanders out of the way, and they're doing their jobs effectively.

Nate approaches as I do, and we enter the room together. It's filled with SWAT guys, but no sign of Scanlon. Morrow's waiting for us.

"He's not here. But at least this time there's no body." He's referring to our previous invasion of the cabin, looking for Phelan.

"What about his stuff?"

"Looks like it's all here. I would say he's coming back."

That immediately sends Nate and me into executing our backup plan. We get the cops outside to disperse, once they've shepherded the bystanders away. We'll leave a few cops hidden to warn us if Scanlon returns, but we want things to look as normal as possible.

The truth is that it's not likely to work; he's probably a savvy guy who will realize something is wrong, if he doesn't already. But it's worth a shot.

"Doug, Nate, come over here," Morrow says. He's by the desk, and when we get to him, he points to it. "We've got good news and bad news," he says. "The good is we've got his computer."

"Great," I say. "What's the bad?"

He points to the garbage can next to the desk. Nate and I look down into it, and there is a cell phone that has been discarded.

"He threw out his cell phone?" I ask. "Why is that a problem?" I'm thinking that it's actually a positive, that maybe we can get information off of it.

"You see the wires attached to it?"

I hadn't noticed that before, but I see it now. There are three or four small wires coming out of the phone. "Yes, what are they?"

"This phone was going to be attached to an explosive device. Calling it would set off an electric charge through those wires and into the device, detonating it."

"So why would he throw it out?"

Morrow shrugs. "We'll find out soon enough."

"And then there was one," I say, and Nate knows exactly what I mean.

We're looking at a body that has been found on the bank of the Pequannock River. I believe it is Rod Scanlon, though that is still to be determined for sure.

Dick Mayer and his adult son were out for a day of fishing when they saw the body. They did not have cell service where they were, so Dick stayed with the body while his son drove to someplace he could call the local police. They came to the scene and immediately notified us, because the victim was killed with a single bullet in the heart.

Nate and I left for the scene immediately, and the local cops have followed our instructions and left everything as they originally found it. Forensics people are doing their work, but basically nothing has changed.

The identity is not a major mystery. The victim's wallet is still in his back pocket, and the identification and other materials are Scanlon's. Other work will be done to confirm identity, including DNA compared to his army record. But the victim looks like Scanlon's photo, with the changes that Alegro Perales described.

I believe it is safe to say that Rod Scanlon is dead and laying at the edge of the water in front of us.

Nate makes the obvious point. "He didn't wash up here; he hasn't been in the water at all."

"No question," I say. "This body was placed here, not thrown in the water. He was meant to be found."

The local cop has told us that it's a fairly popular fishing area, and that there is almost no chance that a decent-weather day could have gone by without it being discovered by someone.

The assistant coroner has been examining the body and comes over to us after he's done so. "I'm Dr. Graham. Ned Graham."

We introduce ourselves and ask him what he's learned so far.

"Well, everything is preliminary, you understand. But I would say that death occurred between fourteen and twenty hours ago. And for various reasons related to lividity, I can say that he was killed elsewhere and the body left here."

I nod. "There's also a lack of blood on the dirt."

"Yes. He was definitely moved, a number of hours after death. That death, of course, was instantaneous."

Our experts have shown up and are examining the scene in detail. There is nothing else for us to do here; we can go back and wait for the medical and forensic results.

On the way back, Nate says, "Phelan wanted us to find him; no doubt about that."

I nod. "He did everything but put up a neon sign with an arrow pointing to the body. But I may have been wrong when I said, 'and then there was one.' I meant Phelan, but there's no way to know if it's just him that is left. There could still be others."

"It seems like being one of Phelan's partners is not a healthy occupation. But why would Phelan have killed him? And more importantly, why would he have wanted us to know Scanlon was dead?"

They're good questions, and while I take a shot at answering them, I could be way off. "Phelan could have killed Scanlon because he went off the reservation, because he was trying to change the rules by which they were playing. And that could have been brought about by the fact that his name went public. I don't think Scanlon expected that; he couldn't have. Because we only picked up on him when Gero died, and Gero's death was not part of their plan."

"Or maybe Phelan didn't want to share whatever the hell the pot of gold is at the end of this rainbow," Nate says.

"Very possible. Also, Scanlon's name becoming public meant he was a potential weak link. Phelan would be afraid that we'd get Scanlon and that he might talk to us. Phelan couldn't have that."

"And getting back to my second question, why would he make it so obvious to us that Scanlon was dead?"

"So we'd stop looking for him, because in looking for him we might come up with something to tie to Phelan."

Nate nods. "Like a cell phone detonator."

"Exactly. And that's the part that worries me the most."

"What is?"

"If Scanlon was building the bomb and probably planting it, then Phelan wouldn't have killed him unless he had already done his job."

"So the bomb is in place."

I nod. "The bomb is in place. It's just sitting there, waiting for the phone call."

There's a new urgency . . . we can all feel it.

It was bad and tense and desperate enough when we were trying to prevent still another citizen from being shot in the heart. Now we are facing the possibility, almost the certainty, of multiple deaths.

Daniel Phelan is going to pick up his phone and dial a number. When it rings on the other end, it will trigger an electric charge that will in turn trigger a device that has been built by Rod Scanlon. That device will then explode, and if it does what its builder intended, it will kill a lot of people.

This morning we're in the FBI building in Newark, in the office of Special Agent Winston Sampson. It's the last place I want to be, and I know that Nate feels the same way. Captain Bradley is here also; he hasn't shared his feelings about it one way or the other.

The meeting, as I fully expected, having been through this on a number of occasions, is the definition of a one-way street. Sampson and his colleagues want us to tell them everything that we know, and have no intention of doing the same.

It's business as usual.

Much to Bradley's surprise when he told us about the meeting, Nate and I are fine with it. For a long while we have been at the point where we want Phelan off the street no matter who makes the arrest, or who takes the credit.

The goddamn KGB can come in and eliminate Phelan, and I'd be fine with it.

So we share everything we have, and Sampson throws us a few crumbs, and it's an hour and twenty minutes that we've wasted. We could have been back at the station or out on the street getting nowhere.

But one thing comes across very clearly: Sampson, and by extension the FBI, is worried. As they should be.

When we get back to the station, we go into Bradley's office, and he calls Jessie in as well. We've become the Gang of Four on this case, most familiar with all aspects of it, and the only people in our department who have been tasked with looking at the big picture rather than just individual parts.

In talking about it, maybe we can see something we haven't seen before.

But when Jessie comes in, she isn't empty-handed. She has some additional information from the search of Scanlon's hotel room. "We cracked his computer," she says. "Unfortunately, he was not a prolific emailer."

"Nothing to work with?" I ask.

"Just one. It was to an email address dph@gmail.com. Doesn't take a genius to know that's likely to be Danny Phelan. There's a subject, but no content. The subject is, 'Mission accomplished . . . I'm on the way.' "

"Was there any reply?"

"No."

"Nothing else?" Bradley asks.

She shakes her head. "We're going through everything, but we've gone back six months already, and there's nothing that could relate to this case. We already have a subpoena out to Google to get all the records from Phelan's email address."

Bradley says, "Demand it immediately, or put the FBI on the case."

She nods. "We'll get it; we explained the life-or-death circumstances."

"Any more from the search?" Nate asks.

"That phone was discarded because the

wire had a nick in it. I assume that rather than repair it and take a chance on it not working, he just had a substitute ready. We got the number off the discarded phone, which shows where it was purchased. It wasn't bought with a credit card, so the store has no record of who made the purchase."

"We know who made the purchase," Nate says. "Scanlon."

"Where was it bought?" I ask. "Maybe he bought the two phones at the same time."

"A convenience store in Lodi."

"That makes sense; that's where he was living. Give me the address; maybe they'll remember."

Jessie gets the address and gives it to me, and Nate and I are off to the store. At the very least it gives us something to do.

"Where the hell were you last week?" The convenience store clerk asks.

"What does that mean?" Nate asks.

"I got robbed last week, at gunpoint. By the time the cops got here, the bastards had time to fly to the Bahamas."

"How much did they get?"

"Two hundred bucks."

Nate frowns. "That won't get you very far in the Bahamas. Is the manager around?"

"Terry Barbaro, at your service."

"You're the manager?"

"And the clerk, and the stock boy, and the bookkeeper. We maintain a fairly low payroll."

I tell him why we're there, and he says, "I'll tell you what I told the cop who called: I looked it up, and the burner phone with that number was paid for in cash."

"And you don't remember the person who bought it?"

"No, sorry. And I don't know how far we're going back here, but I had kids working the register during the summer. One of them could have sold it."

"Could another phone have been bought at the same time? By the same person?"

"It's possible, especially if I wasn't the one who sold it. I think I might remember that."

"Where are the phones you have for sale?" I ask.

"I'll show you," he says, and walks us toward the back. There are at least eight phones of the same make as the one we found in Scanlon's room. The phone numbers are not shown on the packaging.

"We'll take them all," I say. Then, to Nate, "Pay the man."

I grab all the phones from off the rack, and we head back toward the cashier desk. "Why don't you pay for them?" Nate asks.

"All my cash is tied up in equities. Don't worry, if you don't get reimbursed, you'll never have to buy another phone for the rest of your life."

Once we've left and are in the car, Nate asks, "Okay, what the hell was that about?"

"I want to find out whether the phone numbers are in sequence. That way we might be able to narrow down what the number on the second phone might be, the one that's presumably on the device. That is, if Scanlon bought them at the same time."

"How will having the number help us? We can't call it; we'd blow the damn thing ourselves."

"If there's a GPS on it, we can find out where it is."

"Good idea, but we're relying on a lot of 'ifs.' "

I nod. "I'm aware of that."

We get back to the station and start literally tearing the phone packages open. This is not the easiest thing in the world to do; they are made of the same material as DVD cases, which is to say, they are designed never to be opened.

Once we do, we are able to examine the phone numbers and discover that there is some sequence, at least among four of them. The other four numbers are isolated, but that could be because their "mates" had already been sold.

We call Jessie in and tell her what we've discovered, which we're pleased about until she examines one of the phones and breaks the bad news. "No GPS," she says. "Even if we know what number they are going to call, there's no way we can find the phone, or stop it."

"Shit," Nate says. Then, "What are we going to do with these phones?"

"What are you asking me for? They're your phones."

The door opens and a patrolwoman whose name I don't know says, "Sorry to barge in, but we got a hit you're going to be interested in."

"What does that mean?" I ask.

"The tap on James McKinney's phone. Julie Phelan just called him. The call lasted about eighteen seconds."

"Is it on tape?"

She nods. "Of course. You want me to patch it in here? Just take a couple of minutes."

"No. We'll come to you."

"James . . . ," is how she starts the call. He responds, "Julie? Julie where are —"

"James, please listen, I have no time. He took me to Cedar Brook. I need help. . . ."

There's a pause, and McKinney says, "Julie?"

"I have to go . . . he's crazy . . . hurry."

Click.

The voices of Julie Phelan and James McKinney are unmistakable, as is the fear in her voice. Bradley asks to hear it one more time, which of course does not change the content any. If at any point we thought that Julie might be aiding and abetting her father, this effectively removes that possibility. She is a prisoner.

"What is Cedar Brook?" I ask. "Anyone know?"

"It's an all-girls camp near Kinnelon," Jessie says. "My niece Callie went there the last two summers."

"Let's find out everything we can about the layout of the place."

Jessie picks up the phone and tells one of her people what we need, including a Google aerial map.

When she gets off the phone, I ask, "Is there a boys' camp nearby?"

Jessie nods. "I'm sure there is. My niece told me about a dance they had with the brother camp."

"McKinney told me about it when I went to interview Julie Phelan," I say. "That's where they met."

"Let's get a team out there," Bradley says.

I'm about to stand to do just that, when I'm told that McKinney is on the phone for me. "Hello?"

"Lieutenant, Julie just called me. She sounded desperate." I can hear the stress in his voice.

"What did she say?" I want to see if he'll

tell me accurately, though I'm not sure why. It's just some instinct that I have and am giving in to. It turns out that he describes it very accurately.

"That her father is crazy, and that she needs my help. They're at the camp, the camp she went to when . . ."

"What camp is it?"

"Cedar Brook," he says.

"OK. Thank you, we'll take it from here."

"Should I go there?" he asks. "Maybe meet you? I could be there in less than an hour."

"No. We will deal with this. Stay where you are."

"Will you call me and let me know what happens?"

"Yes."

"Please hurry."

I hang up the phone, and Nate says, "Let's go."

"Just a minute," Bradley says, in a tone which indicates he is about to say something important. "I'm bringing in the FBI."

It sounds like challenging him will get nowhere, but Nate does so anyway. "Why would you do that? We can handle this."

"Because they have ten times more assets they can bring to bear than we do. And it is the proper thing to do, procedurally. This is not the time to have a turf war."

"Captain . . . ," Nate starts.

"The decision has been made, Lieutenant."

"Captain," I say, "tell them to have the cell towers shut down in that area. We can't have him making the call and triggering the device."

"Good idea."

Bradley walks out. What he hasn't said is that if this operation goes south, and there is every chance that it will, he doesn't want the blame to fall on his doorstep.

I can't say I blame him, but that's not what I'm focused on right now. I'm too busy replaying in my mind the phone call, and McKinney's description of it.

Bradley goes off to call Special Agent Sampson, and Nate and I prepare to go to summer camp. "I want to go with you," Jessie says.

"No, I need you to check on something for me back here."

"What is it?" she asks, so I tell her.

"Why?" she asks, so I tell her that also.

And then she doesn't argue the point anymore.

Cedar Brook, like every camp in the history of camps, is situated on a lake.

It occupies at least thirty acres and includes six fairly large buildings. According to the maps we are looking at, the buildings are interspersed among outdoor sports facilities including basketball and tennis courts, a pool, and a baseball/soccer field.

It looks like a good place for kids to play in the summer, and a very good place for a crazed murderer to hide once those kids are gone.

There is one main road in the area; it's one lane in each direction. There's a turnoff onto what is called "Camp Road," and as far as I can tell, its existence is merely to provide access from the main road to the camp itself. About three quarters of the way down that mile-long road is a fork, with the road to the right leading to Cedar Brook, and the one on the left leading to Cedar

Hills, the brother camp.

We stop just far enough into Camp Road that we cannot be seen from the main road, and certainly can't be seen from the camp. Sampson and a bunch of agents arrive about ten minutes later. They have maps of the area so detailed, it's as if they had been planning for an invasion of Camp Cedar Brook for years.

Between the FBI agents and our state cops, we have a total of twenty-eight people, all armed and ready to go wherever Sampson tells us. From the moment he arrived he assumed command, and if Bradley is put off by this, he's hiding it very well.

Sampson gathers us around a map. "Theoretically, they could be in any one of the six buildings," Sampson says, "although this first one, here, is the least likely. It's the gymnasium, and there would be no logical reason for them to be there. They need to sleep and eat, and the gym is not the place to do either."

He points again. "These two buildings are the dorms, and this one, the closest to the lake, is the kitchen and eating hall. They would most likely be in one of those three, though we can't take that for granted."

There are trees in plentiful supply throughout the grounds, which will provide some cover, but the immediate areas around the buildings are open space. "If he's watching at all, we'll be seen," I say.

Sampson nods. "There's no way around it, which is why we're going in fast and in force. Our main danger is if he makes the phone call."

"Did you cut off cell service?" Bradley asked.

"There was none to cut off; this is the middle of nowhere. There are no towers in this area. The call would have to be from a landline."

"He's not going to make the call," I say.

Sampson turns to me, obviously surprised. "How do you know that?"

"Because this has been about money all along. And once we're on to him, his chance at the money disappears. Our only real worry is about the hostage, if there is one."

Nate looks at me like I've lost my mind, and I don't go into it any further, but I don't think there is any danger to anyone right now. That boat has sailed.

Of course, I could be wrong about all of it. I won't know for sure until I hear from Jessie. For now, I'm going to follow orders and do what Sampson says.

The plan is for us to approach all six buildings, with more agents assigned to the three likely ones than the other three. It will be done at once and will be a combination of stealth and urgent force. By that I mean we will stay under concealment as long as possible, but once we move, there will be no hesitation.

We will have helicopter support, but it won't appear until the mission is underway, so as not to alert our adversaries.

We will be charging these buildings, leaving ourselves open to fire that I know will not come.

We move on foot down the road toward the camp. Everyone realizes that Phelan could have set up cameras along the route that could easily have been hidden. We disregard the possibility, because there is nothing we could do about it either way.

Sampson sums it up. "If he knows we're coming, he knows we're coming. But we're still coming."

Nate and I are part of the contingent assigned to the mess hall building. If we are to find anyone in any of the buildings, this would seem the most likely one.

We take up our positions in the trees surrounding the building, with all of us able to see the leader of the group, an FBI agent whose name I was told but forgot. He is in communication with the leaders of the other five groups; I'm not sure how, but I have no doubt it's electronically.

When the order is given to move, we will do so simultaneously. We have been told to use all necessary force, though I remain sure that none will be necessary. Of course, I've been wrong before, and this time I hope I am.

We're in place a good ten minutes without an order to move. Everybody is tense, staying silent and unmoving to avoid detection.

And then the order comes, and we move.

I have no way of knowing how the operations at the other buildings are going, but ours goes exactly as planned. There are three doors into the building, and while we are prepared to shoot our way in, all three are unlocked. I hear windows breaking as others in our group take up positions there, to protect us from incoming fire if there are people inside inclined to shoot.

But there are no people inside, at least none that are inclined to shoot.

Danny Phelan and his daughter, Julie, are lying in pools of blood on the floor.

I go over to feel for any pulse either might have. I do Julie first, because Danny's head has essentially been blown off; there is no chance whatsoever that he is alive. Julie is also dead by a means that has become all too familiar: a bullet to the heart.

The scene is set up as a classic murder-suicide, and the weapon lies inches from the fallen Danny Phelan's hand.

It is not a murder-suicide.

That is bullshit.

The agent in charge of our group spreads the word that we are ground zero.

There is a delay before everyone else arrives, no doubt because they are making sure that their buildings are secure, and, in fact, empty.

Sampson takes one look at the bodies of the Phelans and pronounces it a murder suicide, pending forensic confirmation. He wastes no time in calling in a forensics team, now that the danger is gone. He also calls off our air support.

I'm standing off to the side with Bradley and Nate when Sampson approaches. His question is directed squarely at me. "Why would he have done this now?"

I shrug. "Don't know. Must have snapped."

"What did you mean back there when you said, 'This is about the money'?"

Another shrug from me. "What else could it be?"

He's not buying it. "Don't bullshit me."

"Never. I'm respectful of authority. Tell him, Captain."

"He's respectful of authority," Bradley says.

Sampson frowns, seems about to say something negative, and then seems to change his mind in midthought. What comes out is, "You guys can leave whenever."

That's fine with us and Bradley pulls our officers out. As we're walking out I see that there is a pay phone on the wall, no doubt for campers to use to call their parents. It's been a while since I've seen a pay phone.

"Wouldn't have mattered that there's no cell service," I say, pointing to the phone.

Nate says, "A pay phone? It's like going back in time."

Bradley, Nate, and I are going to drive back together, and they are going to pump me for information. And I will give them that information, once I've spoken to Jessie.

When we're on the road, I call Jessie, and she gets on saying, "I was just going to call you. You were right on both counts."

"There's a first time for everything," I say, trying unsuccessfully to sound modest.

"What happened at the camp?"

"Both Phelans are dead. It was made to look like a murder-suicide."

"But we know better," she says.

"Please get started on the next phase."

"Already have; the whole team is on it," she says. "And the warrant has been requested."

"Good. Let me have McKinney's number."

She gives it to me, and I dial it. I had told him I would call when the operation was concluded. I can tell that Bradley and Nate are getting extremely frustrated about being left in the dark.

McKinney answers with, "Lieutenant? What happened? Is Julie okay?"

"I'm afraid she is not. Julie and her father are deceased. I'm sorry to have to tell you this."

"Oh, no . . . God, no."

"The FBI is in control of the scene, but I will let you know when the body can be claimed."

"Thank you."

"Where are you? We will need to conduct a final interview, to memorialize how all of this transpired."

"I'm out of town. I will contact you when I get back. Oh, this is terrible."

I get off the phone and Nate, having heard my end of the call, says, "He didn't ask you how she died."

I nod. "That's because he killed her."

"There are seven hundred and ninety-two companies in the country that write life insurance policies," I say. "I know because I just Googled it."

"So this is about insurance?"

I nod. "Has been from the beginning. When I asked McKinney what he did for a living, he said he was a broker. I assumed stockbroker, but that wasn't the case. Jessie checked; he's an insurance broker."

"You mean like an agent?" Nate asks.

"No, an agent works for a specific insurance company; at least I think that's how it works. A broker can write a policy with any company."

Bradley points out that we had checked into the victims, and with the exception of a small policy that Helen Mizell left, there were no unusual or unexplained insurance issues.

"That's because those people weren't

killed for the insurance money. They were killed to make sure Phelan was seen as the killer. He was set up by McKinney, Gero, and Scanlon. We removed Gero; I'm pretty sure McKinney removed Scanlon."

"How did you know it was McKinney?" Bradley asks.

"What tipped me off initially was the phone call from Julie saying that her father took her to the camp. I know from McKinney that she spent one year at the camp, when she was fourteen. But Phelan left the family when she was twelve and didn't come back for six years. He wouldn't know anything about that camp."

"That's it? There could be other explanations for that."

"I know, but it got me thinking. So I asked Jessie to check a couple of things. Remember when he got that call from Julie from the rest stop on the highway?"

"I do."

"Well, we GPS-checked Julie's phone, which is how we found out she was there. So now I had Jessie GPS-check McKinney's phone to see where he was when he got that call. It turns out he was at the same rest stop; he was standing with her when she made the call.

"He forced her to do it, just like he must

have done at the recent call from the camp. He forced her to make the call, and then he killed them."

"So how were they planning to make money off the insurance?" Bradley asks, and then as he realizes it, he adds, "Damn."

I nod. "Right. Scanlon's explosive device is meant to take out a lot of people, and they already know which people they are. I'll bet that McKinney was setting up insurance policies while Phelan was in prison. This thing takes time; you can't set up a policy and then have the person get murdered the next day; it would cause too much suspicion."

"But won't multiple policies set off suspicion anyway?"

"They wouldn't because it would be spread out. He could have a hundred different policies across a hundred different companies. Don't forget, he had almost eight hundred to choose from. As a broker he could deal with anyone. There would be no reason for any one company having to pay off on a policy that would set off an alarm. It's possible that no single company even holds more than one of the policies for the planned victims."

I continue. "I'll bet the Helen Mizell policy was a practice run just to make sure the process works; he may even have used the fifty grand to pay the premiums on all the other policies. But I'm sure he's got fake names and accounts set up to receive the money. The amount of work involved to construct all this must have been incredible; I'll bet he needed every day that Phelan was in prison."

"How did he know so much about Phelan?" Bradley asks. "He knew all these people that Phelan could have had grudges against."

"I'm sure he got all the information from Julie without her even realizing it. That's why he was with her in the first place."

"So we need to find McKinney," Nate says.

"I'm hoping he'll come in, because he doesn't know we have made him for this. He might want to continue to play the grieving fiancé because if this goes according to his plan, he can continue to live his life out in the open while he collects the money in the dark."

I don't mention that the grieving fiancé role means he'd get mentioned in the obituary, fulfilling one of Jessie's goals for herself.

"You think he'll come in?" Nate asks.

"Not sure. He's smart; he might sense the danger."

"We have to go at this from the other end also," Nate says. "We're reasonably sure the device has been planted; that would have been Scanlon's job, and McKinney wouldn't have killed Scanlon unless the job was done. So if you're right, then this bomb has to go off at a certain time, when certain people are present."

"Right," I say. "Because he has to know which people are going to die; they have to be the people he planned for. And the same people wouldn't be likely to always congregate together. But it could be anywhere . . . a church, a political meeting, the Rotary Club . . . anywhere. But there's a hard time and a hard place."

And we're in a very hard place ourselves.

James McKinney has gone silent.

I've tried to reach him by phone, but the call goes directly to voice mail. This creates a problem greater than just not being able to talk to him; the fact that the phone is shut off means we cannot identify his location by GPS. For all we know the phone could have been discarded or destroyed, and he may be onto another one.

I doubt that he knows we're onto him, though that is a possibility. Until now he has been playing us like an accordion, and I know of nothing that we've done that would make him think he's lost that upper hand.

On one level it might be a good thing for him to know we know his role in this, and I've even considered recommending we go public with it. He would have to understand that our being aware of his plan would make his pulling off the insurance scams much more difficult, if not impossible. It might make him abort the plan.

On the other hand, he could think that some of it would remain salvageable, or even follow through as an act of revenge. I just can't know how his mind works, though I certainly have seen incontrovertible evidence that it does not contain a conscience.

Jessie and I have abandoned any pretense of not talking about work at home; it's our conversational topic every waking minute. It is all-consuming, and intensifies constantly with the knowledge that we are running out of time. Tonight the conversation is pre-dinner, while we're walking Bobo.

"It has to be soon," Jessie points out. "He wouldn't have killed Scanlon, and then especially the Phelans, if that wasn't the case. He was cleaning up all the loose ends. None of them had any remaining value to him, because whatever he was planning was locked and loaded."

She's absolutely right, of course, and there's nothing I can think of to do about it.

I dial McKinney's number again, as I have been doing pretty much every five minutes. As always, it goes directly to voice mail. I don't bother leaving a message, since I've left three already. If he wants to call me back, he will.

Jessie tells me that her people are making no progress on the insurance end of this. With no specific group of people to look for, there is no way to know what insurance policies taken out in the last three years would relate to our case.

"And there are over seven hundred companies to look at," she says. "We'd have to get seven hundred subpoenas, and even then we couldn't do it. We just don't know what we're looking for."

I wish I could make a suggestion that would solve that problem, but I can't. The truth is that the policies that are part of this won't become known until they are about to be paid, which means the people holding them are dead.

"Why did they make the killings look like they were all revenge for petty grudges, other than his ex-wife?" Jessie asks.

"McKinney knew we'd make at least some of the connections; and that it would make Phelan look crazy and capable of anything. He was playing us, and very well. His goal was to make it look like, when the bomb went off, it was consistent with Phelan's behavior."

She shakes her head. "His high school English teacher? That's going back pretty far."

What Jessie just said jogs something in my mind, but I can't get ahold of it. "Julie probably talked about her father a lot, and McKinney would have learned things about his background from her. Maybe he asked Danny Phelan seemingly innocent questions as well."

We get back and Bobo goes right to sleep. He's unconcerned about the case; he's made that clear. I'm still trying to figure out what Jessie said that triggered something still unknown in my mind, but I can't because another awful thing just crowded into it.

"We've got another problem," I say, "and it's a big one."

"What's that?"

"The bomb isn't on a cell phone trigger; it can't be."

"But what about the discarded cell in Scanlon's room, with the wire attached?"

"Maybe that's a backup if the timer doesn't work, but it can't be the only way."

"Why not?"

"Because he killed off Phelan. If the device is shown to be set off by a cell phone, then the dead Mr. Phelan is off the hook, because he's not in shape to dial a phone. McKinney needs to make it look like Phelan planted the bomb, so it can't be a cell phone trigger."

Jessie sees that she has two voice mail messages from people who work for her, and as she retrieves them, I dial McKinney again. Of course it goes straight to voice mail. It's driving me crazy, to the point that I really wish there was a way to hang up a cell phone by slamming it down.

Jessie relays to me what she got in her messages. "The phone call to McKinney from Julie at the camp . . . both her phone and his show it was made and received not at the camp, but about three miles away."

I nod. "There's no cell service there, so they went to the closest place they could find some. There's a pay phone, but he couldn't have her call from there, because he couldn't receive it there, since his phone wouldn't work."

Jessie says something, but I don't hear her and therefore don't respond. "Shit. That's where he is," is what I actually say.

"Where?

"At the camp. That's why I can't get through to him. It's not that he has the phone turned off; it's that he has no cell service."

I stand up. "Jessie, I need you to make two calls for me. One, tell Nate to meet me

at the camp. He can come right in; Mc-
Kinney is not there."

"I thought he was?"

"The second call you need to make is to
your niece, the one who went to Cedar
Brook."

"Callie?"

"If that's her name. Tell her that you know
there's a way that kids could sneak in and
out between the boys and girls camps. I
need to know what that is. Then call me
when you have the answer."

I don't wait for her to respond, because I
know she's got it and will do exactly as I
asked.

The target has to be something unquestionably connected to Phelan.

McKinney wouldn't have taken a chance that we wouldn't be positive that Phelan set the charge before he killed himself. His suicide would have left questions about timing — specifically why would he kill himself before he reached his ultimate revenge, whatever that is?

McKinney would have wanted to avoid those questions by being absolutely sure that we'd blame Phelan, even posthumously. Then McKinney would be off the hook, free to collect the insurance money without any scrutiny.

I can't be positive it's about insurance, but there's no other possibility that I can think of. Bottom line is that at this point, it doesn't matter; we have enough evidence to be sure it's McKinney. We need to catch him and stop that bomb from going off, then later we can figure out his motive.

And I think I know where the bomb is. There is one place, and one place only, that I can think of that is not only definitely tied to Phelan, but also would have a totally predictable group of potential victims present.

Jessie calls me just as I'm reaching for the phone to call her. She says, "Nate's on the way, and I spoke to Callie. She said there is a narrow path in the woods behind the tennis court. It's not obvious; it's only about a foot wide, but once you enter it gets wider. Then it gets smaller at the other end, which is where the boys' camp is. She made me promise I wouldn't tell her mother."

"Good. Jessie, I think I know where the bomb might be set. There is a high school reunion coming up soon for Phelan's class."

"I know; the head of the committee gave you that whole electronic packet, so we would have contact information for Phelan's classmates if we wanted them. I have it on my computer."

"Good. Does it say where and when the reunion is? He told me, but I can't remember."

"Hold on."

She only takes about thirty seconds, but it feels like thirty years. "It's at the Colonnade

Room in Park Ridge; I've been there; they have a banquet hall in the back. And . . . oh, my God . . . it's tonight . . . it's going on now."

"You have got to get everyone out of that restaurant as soon as possible." I have no idea how she can do that, and I'm sort of relieved when she doesn't ask.

"I'm on it," she says, and hangs up.

I am officially scared in a way I can't remember being before. Nate and I are going to do what we have to do; we're good at it, and if it is at all possible, we will get it done.

But at the same time I have just sent Jessie into a situation that is far more dangerous and difficult to deal with. It compounds my anxiety tenfold that I am not going to hear what happened until it is over.

I'm almost as angry as I am scared. All of this was right in front of me, but I couldn't see it until now, when it may be too late.

And Mr. McKinney, I am going to take it out on your ass.

I get to the camp and wait by my car in the parking lot near the main building. Nate arrives ten minutes later, gets out of his car and asks, "What have we got? Jessie called but didn't tell me what is going on. She said she had to call her niece. That was a little weird."

I bring him up to date as quickly and as accurately as I can. I don't tell him why I suspect what has happened, and he doesn't ask. There is time for that later, whether I'm right or wrong.

All he asks is why we are at the girls' camp if we think McKinney is at the boys' version. "Jessie's niece," I say.

Nate and I walk to the tennis courts. We both have our flashlights, so it is not difficult to see the opening in the woods that Callie told Jessie about. It is a foot wide at most, just about big enough for one of Nate's legs.

"We're going to walk through that?" Nate asks.

"It gets wider."

"It better."

The walk through the woods takes about seven minutes, but it feels like a month. All I can think about is Jessie and what she might be doing. I hope it does not include going into that restaurant, but I know that if she thinks it's necessary to do that, she will. She and I are different in one important respect: She's my fiancée, but I sure as hell don't want to be in her obituary.

We finally make it through to the boys'

camp. It is almost identical to the girls' side in that there are the same six buildings, set up the same way, starting with the dining hall closest to the lake. That is the only building with a light on, so I'm certain that's where McKinney is.

That is also the building that, on the girls' side, had the pay phone.

Jessie had no idea how she would accomplish clearing the restaurant.

But she was positive that the first thing she should do is get in the car and drive there. It was about twenty minutes away, and as long as she had her phone with her, she could spend the twenty minutes as productively in the car as at home.

Jessie had always been outstanding under pressure. Things slow down in front of her; she sees situations clearly and acts decisively. That had always come naturally to her, and she had always thought of it as a gift she was lucky to receive.

Now it would matter like it never had before.

Her first call is to the sergeant on call at the station desk. She explains the situation in very few words, but leaves out nothing. He should get every available cop to the restaurant, as well as the bomb squad. And the cops should do whatever is necessary to clear that restaurant of people. The entire call took approximately twenty seconds.

Her next call is to the restaurant to warn them. At first she planned to identify herself, explain the situation, and insist that they evacuate. As the woman at the restaurant is answering and Jessie is about to open her mouth, she changes her mind.

There is just no time to follow the proper procedure. She is going to do something that could get her into trouble, but the possible alternative is too grim to contemplate.

"Listen, you son of a bitch bastard," she says, in as harsh a tone as she can muster. "I've set a bomb to go off in your restaurant in seven minutes. You hear me? Seven minutes! Your ass is mine! The revolution is here!"

Click.

Our flashlights are off as we head for the building.

It's easy to find our way, there's enough moonlight to allow us to see quite well. Of course, that same moonlight would let McKinney see us approaching, and that will get even worse when we get close enough for the light of the building to illuminate us even more.

But we can't worry about that now; this is no time for subtlety. We are here to take him down, not play games.

Our plan is for Nate to take the back door while I take the side door. That will bring me into the area just outside the kitchen, where the pay phone was in the girls' building. Everything else so far has been the same, so I hope and assume this is no different. Although I obviously would rather there is no pay phone here at all.

I slowly turn the doorknob and find out

that it is unlocked. In fact, there may not be a lock on it at all; there would be no reason to worry about a thief entering a camp dining hall. The food is generally not that good.

But I'm going to have to open the door, slowly and carefully, and there is a strong likelihood that it is going to squeak or make noise in some fashion. There is no way around that, and it is still preferable to bursting in without knowing what is on the other side.

With my handgun in my right hand, I use my left to open the door as slowly and quietly as I can, scanning the room as more of it comes into my line of sight.

"Good evening, Lieutenant. Welcome to the dining hall," McKinney says. "Party of one?"

He is sitting on a stool at the pay phone. He has a gun in one hand, and his other one is poised over the push buttons. "I'm going to assume you know quite a bit if you took the trouble to join me here tonight. I've dialed six of the seven digits; I further assume you know what happens if I dial the seventh."

The reservations clerk at the restaurant was not quite as calm in a crisis as Jessie.

Her initial reaction was to scream and start to cry uncontrollably. The scream might have been loud enough to attract the attention of the manager if he was in Connecticut, but that wasn't necessary, since he was about five feet away from her.

"She said there's a bomb in here . . . in seven minutes! She said we're all going to die!"

"Take it easy. Who said that?"

"Some lady! She was horrible. She said there's a bomb in seven minutes, and we're all going to die in a revolution!"

This is the first time the manager had ever faced this situation, and it was certainly an inopportune time. The restaurant was packed, and there was a class reunion party in the banquet room.

But while he never had to deal with this

before, he had undergone sufficient training for all kinds of emergencies, from bomb scares to live shootings. There was no doubt what he had to do, regardless of the unpleasantness it caused his patrons. He was not afraid of a potential bomb; the chance that the threat was real was quite small. But failure to do what he had been instructed to do could cost him his job, and that he was afraid of.

There was an interior alarm in the restaurant, planned mostly for fire alerts, but which could be manually triggered. He set it off, causing a high-pitched intermittent series of audio blasts.

"Ladies and gentleman, everybody please get up and leave the restaurant in an orderly fashion! Please, carefully and safely, but you must leave now. This is an emergency!"

The waitstaff, similarly trained in these procedures, started to clear patrons from the restaurant, even though most of them had no idea why. The ones assigned to the reunion banquet went into that room to get those people to leave as well.

The patrons, worried but not understanding, did not move as quickly as instructed. Some went back for their handbags, some resentfully delayed simply because they did not want their dinner interrupted. The slower they moved, the more insistent the restaurant employees became.

No one had any idea how little time was left.

"There are fifty cops outside this building," I say.

McKinney laughs in response. "Right, but they sent you in alone. I can then only assume your colleagues must agree with me that you are very unlikable."

"They think I can talk some sense into you. There's nothing to gain by keeping this going."

"I'll feel more comfortable continuing this conversation with your gun on the floor, Lieutenant. Now."

"You do the same."

"Lieutenant . . . ," he says. His tone is warning, but the fact that he moves his hand closer to the phone in a threatening manner is motivating. I put my gun on the floor.

"Nicely done," he says. "And you're wrong; I have everything to gain. You think you know everything, but you know nothing."

Nate, where the hell are you?

"I know that you killed Danny Phelan, and Julie Phelan, and either killed or directed the murder of all the others."

He smiles, then looks quickly at his watch. "And do you know why?"

I'm torn here. If I say that I know about the insurance scheme, he will have to assume I've told others, and that his plan will never work. It might cause him to dial that last number in anger, or even more likely, shoot me.

If I pretend not to know his plan, then maybe I can keep this conversation going for a while, at least until my enormous goddamn partner can manage to get in here. His door was probably locked, and he's no doubt trying to find another way in without making noise.

"I know all about your ridiculous insurance scam, you sack of shit," I say, changing my mind in the moment. I can see him react, flinching as the realization hits him.

I continue, "The whole world knows about it. You press that button and that whole world will track you down; there will be nowhere for you to escape. Don't do it and you can walk out of here and get under whatever rock you planned to hide under."

He looks at his watch again, and for the

first time I can see worry in his face. If I'm right, then he has no control over what is going to happen; he can detonate the bomb with a phone call, but he has no way to prevent the timer from detonating it on its own.

The next look on his face tells me that I've misjudged the situation. He knows the bomb will go off, and that he will have to run. So he wants to do it now, and he wants to do it without me being around to witness it and talk about it.

"Goodbye, Lieutenant, I need to be going."

He raises his gun to fire, and I dive to the left as the shot goes off. I look up to see that the shot was not fired by McKinney at all, but by Nate. McKinney won't be cashing any insurance checks, ever again.

Nate walks toward me, obviously pleased with himself.

"Where the hell were you that it took you so long? Going for a swim?" I ask.

"We're even," he says.

"Yes, we are," I say, and I go to the pay phone to find out what is happening at the reunion.

Jessie is very relieved to find what looks like two hundred people outside the restaurant.

She pulls her car as close as she can get; which is adjacent to three state police cars already there. She runs toward the restaurant, screaming at the cops, "Is everybody out?"

Suddenly she hears a woman yell, "My husband is still in there."

Without so much as pausing, Jessie continues running into the restaurant. Once inside, she doesn't see anyone, and runs from room to room yelling, looking for anyone left behind.

She still sees no one and, thinking the woman must have gotten separated from her husband in the chaos, goes toward the exit. As she passes the men's room, the door opens and Morris Feldman, a sixty-seven-year-old grandfather of four, comes out. He looks around, bewildered, at the restaurant, entirely empty except for Jessie. "Where is everybody?"

"Come on, we've got to get out," Jessie yells, grabbing Morris by the hand. They run out the door, her pulling him on his arm, but his legs unable to match her speed.

They run toward the cops and patrons, all standing along a perimeter about fifty yards away. They've gone twenty of those yards when the building behind them explodes, the impact hurling them to the ground.

Some small shards of glass hit them in the back, causing bloody but not life-threatening injuries. Jessie turns to her running mate and says, "What's your name?"

He is obviously shaken and in some pain, but manages, "Morris."

She nods. "Morris, if I were you, I wouldn't leave a tip."

Jessie and Morris stay in the hospital for two days.

Luckily for them, the glass shards did not do significant damage, but the cuts are fairly deep, and they need to be on IV antibiotics to ward off potential infection.

I visit her as much as I can, though the aftermath of the McKinney situation forces me to be in the office most of the time. I also have to spend some time caring for Bobo, who stares continuously at me as if to say, "If you did anything to my mother, your ass is mine."

Not much has come out to shed any further light on the situation; McKinney is the one who knows all the answers, and he won't be doing any more talking.

But I've thought about it, and I think I know what precipitated Gero taking a shot at me, and McKinney capturing Julie and keeping her imprisoned with her father. I think that all happened when Julie promised that she would give me some of her father's papers. There must be something in there that would have somehow tipped us off.

We haven't tracked those papers down yet to whatever storage area Julie had them in, but eventually we will, and maybe we'll learn more.

We've also learned from the amazing Lieutenant Anderson that McKinney was the one transferred into the unit when Phelan went out. That was the "trade." So while Phelan would not have known McKinney, that's how McKinney came to know Gero and Scanlon.

The entire case has left me shaken in a way that Jessie and Nate would say is inconsistent with the "old me." I think that is partially because of the danger I sent Jessie into; I don't know how I could ever have dealt with it if something terrible had happened.

Mixed in with all this is tangible relief that Phelan turned out not to have been the guilty party. It means that my letting him off the hook for Brookings was not the cause of the subsequent deaths.

Jessie is being hailed by the media as a hero, and rightfully so. She saved a lot of people with some damn quick thinking. And my guess is she'll be crowned Queen of the Reunion.

When I go to pick her up to bring her home, I get a little emotional and even discover a lump in my throat. It's not a feeling I've often experienced.

"Jessie, I don't know what I —"

She cuts me off. "We're a pretty damn good team," she says.

Yeah, we are.

I'm attending an evening gathering to honor Danny and Julie Phelan.

In my experience, it's the first memorial event held in a sports bar, but Andy Carpenter is hosting it and no doubt paying for it. Not surprisingly, it's at Charlie's, his favorite hangout, so it will also have the best French fries and beer in the history of memorial tributes.

I haven't spoken to Andy since the Phelans were killed. He comes over to me as soon as I enter and says, "Welcome. Glad you could make it."

"Interesting choice of venues."

"Actually, Danny and I had all our meetings here; he loved the burgers. I think he would approve of the choice. And Julie would have happily gone along with anything her father wanted."

"I'm sorry it had to end the way it did," I say.

He nods. "Me, too. They were good people who could have used better breaks along the way."

Andy had been telling me all along that Danny was innocent, but he's not throwing in any I told you sos now. I respect and appreciate that, even coming from a defense attorney.

I see Pete Stanton and Vince Sanders at their regular table, eating and drinking. "How come they're here?" I ask. "Did they even know the Phelans?"

"Doesn't matter," Andy says. "They would have attended services for Osama bin Laden if the beer and food were free."

"Let me ask you something," I say. "I think McKinney was worried that Julie was going to turn over some of Danny's papers that she had in storage. It worried him enough to precipitate his capturing her and taking a shot at me. You have any idea what that could have been about?"

He thinks for a moment and then says, "I'm not sure, but Danny had been in and out of drug treatment for a very long time. A therapist once told him that keeping a daily journal would help him 'stay in the moment,' whatever the hell that means. But he did it for many years."

"Interesting, but still doesn't tell me

what's in there."

"Could have been his relationship with Gero and Scanlon, which had been bad ever since the army. They thought Danny ratted them out on some drug stuff. He didn't, but that's why he was willing to leave that unit."

"I wish I would have known that," I say.

"Would it have changed things?"

"Probably not."

"Then have a beer and toast their memory. And don't beat yourself up. You did good," he says, and then adds, "For a cop."

ABOUT THE AUTHOR

David Rosenfelt is the Edgar and Shamus Award-nominated author of nine stand-alones and sixteen previous Andy Carpenter novels, most recently *Collared*. He and his wife live in Maine with twenty-seven golden retrievers that they've rescued.

The employees of Thorndike Press hope you have enjoyed this Large Print book. All our Thorndike, Wheeler, and Kennebec Large Print titles are designed for easy reading, and all our books are made to last. Other Thorndike Press Large Print books are available at your library, through selected bookstores, or directly from us.

For information about titles, please call:
 (800) 223-1244

or visit our website at:
 gale.com/thorndike

To share your comments, please write:
 Publisher
 Thorndike Press
 10 Water St., Suite 310
 Waterville, ME 04901